the other side of youth

the other side of youth

stories by **Kelli Deeth**

ARSENAL PULP PRESS

VANCOUVER

ARSENAL PULP PRESS
Suite 202–211 East Georgia St.
Vancouver, BC V6A 1Z6
Canada
arsenalpulp.com

The publisher gratefully acknowledges the support of the Canada Council for the Arts and the British Columbia Arts Council for its publishing program, and the Government of Canada (through the Canada Book Fund) and the Government of British Columbia (through the Book Publishing Tax Credit Program) for its publishing activities.

Earlier versions of some of these stories have appeared in the following publications: "The Things They Said" in *Joyland*; "Embrace" in *Event*; "End of Summer" in *The New Quarterly*; "A Boy's Hand" in *The Puritan*; "Souvenirs" in *The Rusty Toque*; and "Ari" in *The Dalhousie Review*.

This is a work of fiction. Any resemblance of characters to persons either living or deceased is purely coincidental.

Cover photograph by Eleonora Ghioldi/Blend Images/Corbis
Editing by Susan Safyan
Book design by Gerilee McBride

Printed and bound in Canada

Library and Archives Canada Cataloguing in Publication

Deeth, Kelli, author
    The other side of youth / Kelli Deeth.

Issued in print and electronic formats.
ISBN 978-1-55152-523-5 (pbk.).—ISBN 978-1-55152-524-2 (epub)

    I. Title.

PS8557.E326O74 2013   C813'.6   C2013-903259-2
                                                C2013-903260-6

For Liam

Contents

The Things They Said

COURTNEY PEERED INTO THE rearview mirror, and Michael was gone. She knew he hadn't abandoned her, that he had only gone in to pay for the gas, but that kind of sudden disappearance grabbed her in a delicate spot in the lining of her stomach. And then, just as suddenly, the thunk of the door opening and the huge, firing electricity of his presence. It was early in the morning, and she felt things more.

They had crossed into Colorado in the dark, so she was just beginning to see it, the hardness of it. They were on their way to Michael's stepfather's funeral in Parker.

"All done?" she said. She turned the ignition, then rested her hand on the gear shift.

"All done."

Michael squeezed her hand with his strong, warm fingers. She liked it when her hand was taken suddenly; it relieved her of some stress she wasn't aware of until it drained away.

When they were on the highway again, Courtney said, "I want you to stay awake."

"Why do you need me to stay awake?"

"I stayed awake for you," she said, though she could not account for long stretches of the night. She remembered trying to knit a scarf and then simply thinking. Had she been born the way she was, or had she been created by circumstance and necessity? What would it be like to have a different name? She had asked Michael, "If you didn't know me, what would you think my name was?" At first, he didn't want to play the game, but when she persisted, wouldn't let it drop, he said, "I would think it was Naomi." But she knew that was his favourite name—his answer had nothing to do with her.

She added, "I don't like driving alone."

"You're completely capable of driving alone." But Michael reached into the compartment between the seats and pulled out his Plutarch, *Makers of Rome*.

"What's Plutarch talking about now?" Courtney said.

"Same old." Michael put the book face-down in his lap. "I was just thinking," he said.

"Thinking what?"

"That we're going to be okay."

"Are things not okay?"

"You know what I mean."

A couple of weeks ago, Courtney told Michael that every decision she had ever made had been the wrong one, and that she didn't know what the right ones were. The main decisions of her adulthood had been to earn a master's degree in philosophy, to marry Michael, and to never bear children. She couldn't say what exactly was wrong with her choices, only that she was beginning to feel buried. What she said was cruel, but Michael held her and let her grieve her mysterious grief.

"Do you believe me?" Michael said.

"I believe you," she said, because it was the only thing to say. Although all of her decisions had been the wrong ones, she could not exist without Michael.

He began to read to her, which he did to stay awake. His voice was bold but sensitive, like someone reading on the radio. She was sure that if he had lived a thousand years earlier, he would have been an orator, wandering dusty streets, beloved of his followers.

They arrived at the hotel in the middle of the afternoon.

Courtney turned on the television, found a tennis match, then sat on the end of the bed. There was the sound of water pouring into the tub—Michael always took a bath after car trips. Finally, the water stopped. The tennis match had almost hypnotized Courtney.

"Courtney?" Michael called.

She waited for him to call her again.

"Courtney," he called again. "Get in here."

His voice pulled her to a standing position. She found herself stepping stiffly toward the bathroom.

She sat on the toilet seat lid and watched him take his bath, as he liked her to do at home. It was one of the times he did not like to be alone.

"What's going on?" Michael said.

"I was watching tennis." Michael's short, dark hair was wet, and when it was wet, she could see more clearly that he was balding and the bright, almost babyish pink of his scalp. His nose looked bigger, too; the end, which lifted up slightly, was more bulbous.

"You don't like tennis," he said.

"When I was younger, my dad wanted me to be a pro, but I was too lazy to practice that hard." But after she said it, she realized that really she had longed to disappoint him, to become a problem he would have to endlessly solve.

"You never told me that."

"I never thought about it until now."

"So he wanted you to be a pro."

"He got it into his head that I would be good at it, and I pretended to like it."

"Your dad's an asshole."

"Why does that make him an asshole?"

"He should have asked you what you wanted to be."

"I never wanted to be anything," she said. "That was my problem.

He was trying to help me." But she didn't want to talk about that—her confusion, her sadness, how she felt her father had failed her.

"I like it here," she said. The low mountains perturbed her at first, but now they began to pull her, as if by some peculiar, horizontal gravity.

After the bath, Michael and Courtney lay on their separate sides of the bed. Sunlight pressed at the curtains, but Courtney insisted that both of them lie down and rest before dinner, since they had been up all night. She didn't want Michael falling asleep early, when she would probably still be up, feeling her blood move at a quicker pace.

Something else was on television now, a documentary about Picasso. On the screen, briefly, was a painting of a woman and a young child, both figures contorted with longing. She could not hear the commentary, and then the image disappeared. Now a man sat in a chair and spoke to an invisible interviewer. Courtney reached over Michael's body, found the remote on his night table, and pointed it at the screen, pressing the red power button. The quiet room buzzed around her. Courtney couldn't sleep or rest without the television. When she was younger, she had lived her life downstairs in front of the television while her mother had lived upstairs in the living room. Her father had lived somewhere else. Why was Courtney thinking about her father? He wasn't ill, and he wasn't so old yet that she had to worry about him having a heart attack. But lately, when she was doing the dishes or on the subway to work, she wondered how she would feel if he died, if she would feel like something had been ripped away from her, or if she would feel nothing, because he hadn't lived with her, and "father" was only a word. Her friends had had fathers who lived at home, so she knew what they looked and sounded like. They shaved in the mornings, they reached into their pockets for money, they handed over car keys with warnings, they said: You be home on time; You listen to your mother; You're going to get it. Courtney's father was something else—a distant participant in her life, dropping her off and driving away to the tenth-floor apartment where he lived alone; he was a man who had helped her into the world but who was not a father. In the summer, he would pull up in her driveway in his white tennis shorts and red polo shirt. For a couple of hours on the court, he became her fierce, unmerciful opponent, but she had difficulty becoming his. When she spiked her balls out of bounds and then stood there limply, defeated, he would shake his head and say she was like her mother. She had the physique and stamina for tennis, he said, but she didn't even try. Afterwards, she sat in the passenger seat, silent and guilty as he gave her tips on serving. Within minutes, they parted like—like what?

Courtney got up quietly, went to the window, and pulled the harsh blue curtain open. Their room was at the back of the hotel, so she had a view of the almost empty parking lot. All through the trip, she worried that the car would be stolen. The rented blue Nissan still sat among three pickup trucks. In Toronto, she hardly ever saw pickup trucks and more often saw gleaming cars that she and Michael couldn't afford. Trees blocked her view of the strange, arid, reddish mountains that penetrated her mind early this morning. She didn't want to go to the funeral. Michael's mother, Elizabeth, would look for ways to hurt her, as she always did. And Courtney didn't want to see a dead man. Even though the death of his stepfather was no great loss for Michael and no loss at all for Courtney, the necessity of attending his funeral and facing his corpse had done something to her, shaken her, caught her at an angle where she was surprised to find she bled. People you might never have found the energy to love died, before you were ready. Her father would one day die, without ever having become, in Courtney's mind, a father. Her only hope for a normal mourning was to somehow deceive herself.

"What do you say?" Michael said.

Courtney jumped, then she turned. Michael was on his back, smiling.

Courtney said, "Sure." She was tired, but she didn't want to miss an opportunity to be close to him; he gave off heat, and her skin drew it in, held it for hours afterward.

Courtney and Michael were driving to the steakhouse, even though they could see it from the parking lot of the hotel. The sign, RICK'S STEAKHOUSE, written in orange flames, revolved, slightly turning Courtney's stomach. Still, there was something about this place, the dry evening warmth, the almost disgusting amount of sun, that gave her hope for something she couldn't quite put her finger on.

Their waiter was a teenage boy. His name tag said Justin, which was a name Courtney liked, with its suggestions of dignity and self-control. First, he brought them water and bread. Courtney studied his forearms; he was not a child, but he was not a man. His forearms were thin but muscular, lightly haired. Courtney experienced the soft yet crushing maternal feeling she always did around a boy or girl she might have been the mother of.

When the waiter left, Michael tilted his head and looked at her and then put his elbows on the table, bringing his hands together. He studied her face, as if preparing himself for something, anything, she might say. But Courtney didn't need to point out that they were out of place at the restaurant—they'd been through that. Others Courtney and Michael's age had children who were six or seven years old, children who would be teenagers by the time Courtney and Michael were in their early forties. She thought a lot about numbers and her personal timeline. Eight was the year she learned to never trust a feeling of peace. Twenty-seven was the year she met Michael. Forty was to come, then fifty, then anything or nothing, depending on the unknown will of her body. Thirty-seven was the year in which her decision could still be unmade, reborn as something shocking and unrecognizable, like the brightness of the sun today. But Courtney had made the decision; it took everything she had to take care of herself—the child would starve, and she would watch it starve, as her mother and father had watched her starve. Courtney and Michael weren't career people. Courtney worked in human resources at an engineering firm, and Michael fixed computers. They hadn't chosen childlessness in exchange for money and power and prestige; Courtney hadn't been able to bring herself to go off the pill, to allow the worm of a pregnancy, the stream of hormones.

"I was thinking I could live here," Courtney said.

"Why on earth would you want to live here?"

Courtney stared at him, her lips pressed together. Then she said, "Maybe a shake-up is what people need sometimes."

"Does this have anything to do with all your bad decisions?"

Their wine came. The waiter—Justin—was smiling, a secret, completely pleased smile that couldn't have had anything to do with Courtney and Michael. When Courtney was a teenager, she had worked in a lighting store and wandered in and around the lamps, thinking about sex.

After he poured their wine, Justin stood with his notepad. Michael ordered steak and Courtney ordered spaghetti, something she craved every couple of weeks.

He took their menus. He glanced at Courtney, a blank, unseeing glance. She was used to them, but not quite. The glances left her wanting to say something that nobody would stay and listen to, that she was an adult woman, not a defect, a chipped vase there was no place for on any shelf.

When he was gone, Courtney studied the tablecloth. It was white, with wings embroidered into it. She moved her eyes from one pair of outstretched wings to another.

"You look like you lost your best friend," Michael said.

"Everything's fine. I've made my decisions."

"Yes, you have."

She straightened, and the muscles in her back were full of dull pain.

"What you need," Michael said. "What you need is to stop thinking you're worthless."

"I don't think I'm worthless."

"It's like you're constantly telling the world that you don't deserve anything."

"All I said is that I might want to live here. Your mother moved here."

"My mother's also crazy, not to mention a raging alcoholic."

"I feel what I feel," Courtney said. "How can I help that?"

After a few minutes, Justin came with their plates of food. Michael cut into his steak, put a piece in his mouth, and chewed precisely. Courtney had lost her appetite. The spaghetti was a grotesque heap.

"What's the matter?" Michael said.

"Nothing at all is the matter," Courtney said. "And I don't think I'm worthless."

"You want to live here, we'll live here," Michael said. "We'll leave all our problems behind. Ride off into the sunset. That's what you want?"

"Maybe there was never any decision to make," Courtney said. "Maybe I never had a choice about anything." She looked up and off into a chandelier hanging across the room; there was the perfect, awful rightness of what she had said.

Michael stared at her. "That's the most ridiculous thing I've ever heard," he said. He cut into his steak again. "But if that's the way you feel."

"I had a choice about you," she said, even though, in the way she needed and loved, she hadn't. As the months of their courtship went by, she grew more and more attached, hooking her arm into his on walks to and from restaurants, not letting him leave on Sunday night.

"Whatever you say."

Justin came and asked politely if everything was okay, and Courtney smiled and nodded and told him it was. He lent a temporary, almost burning warmth, and she wished he would stand there for a minute, so she could pretend to have ownership, so she could pretend that she had let herself be cut open, and then doted on him, never falling into her own blackness, the shadow of being eight years old. He left, and she couldn't watch him leave. She could never stand the sight of someone's back, getting farther away, the sight of someone leaving her cold. Watching meant she was admitting the departure was happening, feeling and knowing the quiet terror of it. When she looked at Michael, she saw that his eyes were wet. She said his name, but he would not look at her. "Michael?" she said again, and he put another piece of steak into his mouth.

The hotel room felt like a box, too square, too severe. The walls pressed in and around Courtney, as they sometimes did at home, in the apartment.

Courtney and Michael leaned back against their individual pillows and watched television, a show Michael had put on. Three men and one woman, all in suits, debated at a round table, their hands fluttering, their mouths tensing and twitching, their shoulders bracing. On the short drive back to the hotel, she and Michael hadn't spoken, not with words, not out loud. But messages, as always, were passed back and forth between them. Michael, she knew, was sick of going over ground they had already gone over, opening cases that had been concluded. She had made the decision, and he respected it. In fact, he felt the same way she did; he didn't want to raise a child if Courtney didn't feel she could be a good mother to it, if she didn't really want it deep down. He promised her he did not love her any less. But Courtney could say to all of that, "What if I can't grow up?" She could say, "I don't believe you."

Michael changed channels without consulting her, and Courtney didn't argue.

In a couple of days, they would attend the funeral. Parkinson's had controlled the man's body for years. Michael had never really known his stepfather because his mother had met him through a personal ad after she moved to Colorado. She had left her job in London, Ontario, because she wanted to show Michael's father, who had gone on to have another family, that she had moved on, too. She dated and then married a man she knew would become immobile. The alcoholism had been there since Michael was four, a fact and nothing more, the terrible weather of his past, his young life. Elizabeth still called when she was drunk to tell him that she was lonely, that Bob was killing her, but since living with Courtney, Michael was getting better at not answering the phone and at waiting days or weeks to call back.

For two days, Courtney and Michael had travelled together to go somewhere neither of them wanted to go, but had no choice, because Michael's mother, no matter how much she had wounded and neglected Michael—Elizabeth had once beaten him with a towel rack—was still his mother. Courtney would be an observer at the funeral, and the most she would feel was pity. She had decided long ago that when it came to his mother, she would feel nothing else. When Courtney first met Elizabeth, she had been amazed at her pale, smooth skin, her blue eyes, magnified by her glasses. In her lilac pantsuit, she hadn't seemed like someone who had chased Michael, the curly-headed child, around the house, telling him his father never loved him. She had seemed like an elegant lady, delicate and fragile. She had reminded Courtney of her grandmother, who had gone to church every Sunday. After coming back to the apartment from the restaurant, Elizabeth and Michael drank together on the balcony while Courtney had watched a biography about Katherine Mansfield on TV and then tried to read Romantic poetry from an anthology she had bought for a class. She had finally gone into their bedroom. She was surprised to see Michael a few minutes later, coming to bed and thanking her for giving him an excuse to leave his mother. Once they were both under the covers, Elizabeth opened their bedroom door and sat at the foot of the bed. She told Courtney not to feel bad that she was barren, that this was what happened to many women, and that it was a blessing, really, when so many intelligent women became nothing but breeders. Courtney, who didn't know then that there was no point in arguing with a drunk, said frankly that she wasn't barren, that she and Michael had made a choice. His mother looked at Michael and asked, "Is this true? You people chose to live this way?"

Then Courtney told her to get out of their room. Elizabeth stared at Courtney, then stood and left the room. When the door to the second bedroom (their office, with an air mattress on the floor) closed, Michael had asked, "Did you have to be so mean?"

"Didn't you hear what she said to me?"

"I heard what she said to you."

Instead of reading, he turned out his light. It was only later that Courtney realized—and the realization came out of nowhere when she was paying for groceries—that Michael had told his mother that Courtney was barren to save them both from her disapproval, to make Courtney look tragic, to ensure warm tides of sympathy.

Since then, no matter how much his mother wept into the phone, Courtney asked herself who such a mother was to even imagine that she had been a mother.

Courtney adjusted the pillow so she was sitting up straighter, and Michael went to the bathroom. He had an elaborate before-bed ritual. He brushed his teeth, flossed, washed his face with a hypo-allergenic soap, plucked any hair to be found in his nose and ears, then applied lotion to his shoulders, where his skin broke out in small, red pimples. Courtney was relieved that she and Michael had had sex earlier, because she didn't want to now. If they argued, even if silently, her naked body felt too vulnerable near his.

Courtney looked up at the ceiling. There was an oval light fixture with a pattern of curled-up daisies on it. She tried to imagine that her father was already dead, that the news had come. If she could feel sadness, that would mean he amounted to a father and she amounted to a daughter, and that the hollowness she knew of as her self was only a memory, a brief experience, and that really she had lost nothing. She experienced a sensation of impatience as she waited to experience a sensation; then she curled up, like one of the etched daisies.

When Michael emerged from the bathroom, he said, "I was a dick earlier."

"No, you weren't. I knew it was crazy. I just wanted to tell someone I had had the thought."

"It wasn't crazy," he said. "You're just sick of things. Everyone gets sick of things." Then he said, "It's not over until it's over, you know."

"It's over for me," Courtney said.

"You mean, the fat lady has sung?"

She wasn't going to tell him again why she couldn't allow a child to be abandoned, to grow up like she had. She had been lucky to find Michael.

"There's lots to enjoy in this world," Michael said. "We're not going to be like everyone else."

"It's not because I want that," Courtney said. "I don't mind everyone else. I like them."

Michael took off his jeans and his shirt. He was turned away from her, facing the cabinet that held the coffee maker and the bowl of chocolate bars and other snacks, and where Michael had rested the two electronic cards that served as keys to the room. Michael's back was long and muscular, like a male dancer's. She couldn't see them now, but she knew from past exploration that Michael had small white scars all along his spine. He said he wasn't aware of them, and that he didn't know how he had gotten them. One of the lies between them. Courtney lied too. She knew that she and Michael were joined, and that where she took him, he had no choice but to go because he didn't insist on anything.

Michael stood before her in his boxer shorts.

"Sometimes I think you'd be better off without me," he said. He flicked out the overhead light, so the room was dark except for a glow from the parking lot that washed up against the curtains.

Courtney pulled her knees up. He always said this, that he was an anchor, pulling her down. Another man, he told her, would have cured her of her uneasiness. Her answer, after all these years of trying to convince him otherwise, was no answer.

Michael got into bed.

Courtney was still on top of the covers. She sat there, her arms wrapped around her knees. Michael quickly fell asleep, as he usually did after turning off the light. His congested, jagged breathing gave his unconsciousness away. If she wanted to talk to him, she had to begin the conversation when the light was on; in sleep, he was irretrievable.

Courtney looked at Michael's bare shoulders, pale and soft in the light from the parking lot. She wondered if she had robbed herself and Michael of what most people seemed to live for, and all most people attained in the end, the simple joy of their children's painful need for them. The thoughts lit up her brain.

She crept over to the window, pulled back the curtain a little. The car was still there. She had bothered Michael the entire trip with her irrational fear that their rented Nissan would be stolen. Michael told her that if it was stolen, they would manage. He would manage. But in her mind, she and Michael would be thrown into chaos.

As she stood there, she could almost hear Michael's voice, a firm voice that shook when he was upset. He would tell her to be happy with who she was, to hold her head up, to be proud of the choices she had made, because she had made them with her own well-being in mind. She and Michael were a family, and who was to say they were not? They were a family like anyone else; no one was missing, no one was wanted, no one would leave the other, and no one would be left alone to fend for themselves. The things they said to each other, over and over; words whose meanings brought little comfort, no matter how beautiful and logical they were, no matter how often they were said, who said them or who heard them, whose voice trembled or whose broke.

End of Summer

ON HER WAY THROUGH the rain to Ingrid's, Sandra passed the field. An older man walked his dogs across it, seeming to have no idea what sometimes went on there.

Ingrid's house blinked into view. Ingrid wanted to break up with Tom today, and she wanted Sandra's help. Tom was thirty-six.

Ingrid's mother, a secretary in Scarborough, wasn't home, and the rule was that Sandra could walk right in.

Triumph blared—"Lay It on the Line." In the living room on the couch, Ingrid's older brother, whose arms were too short for his body, smoked a fat joint with the tallest boy in the neighbourhood, Eddie, who had curly hair and skinny lips. Before he had killed himself a year ago, Sandra's brother had supplied them with pot from plants he grew in his bedroom closet.

"Sniffer's almost ready," her brother said. He and his friends called Ingrid Sniffer after he'd claimed to catch her smelling her mother's underwear last year in grade seven. Ingrid always said it wasn't true.

Sandra pushed open Ingrid's bedroom door and found her baby-powdering the insides of her thighs. She wore a white sundress, nylons, and a pair of her mother's black high heels. Two yellow ribbons dangled from either side of her head. The baby powder container exhaled as she set it on the dresser beside her three glass unicorns that faced each other in a circle—a gift from her father.

Ingrid was the only one allowed to touch the unicorns.

"You're going to get soaked in that," Sandra said, following Ingrid to the front hall.

"So?" Ingrid said. She grabbed a beige dress coat with a belt from the front hall closet, and her hands vanished into the sleeves.

"Whose is that?"

"Mum's. Gave it to me."

"Why are you so dressed up if you're going to break up with him?"

"Doesn't hurt to dress up once in a while, Bitch." Sometimes they called each other Bitch instead of by their names. It didn't mean they weren't friends.

Ingrid grabbed an umbrella from a hook beside the closet, then pushed open the screen door. The rain was even heavier. Sandra pulled the hood of her rain coat up. Ingrid's heels snagged the pavement.

They plodded through the schoolyard, and the rain on Sandra's face felt like sharp, cold pins. Ingrid didn't share the umbrella. By the time they stopped at the store, the rain had stopped and the sun was coming out. That always happened in summer.

Sandra yanked open the door and pushed herself in. Two little boys were picking out bags of chips. Ingrid went and stood by the candy and chocolate bars, reading ingredients because she was allergic to flour. Sandra vibrated with the need to humiliate Forehead, the young man who worked behind the counter. He didn't care that he was ugly and weak. The feeling was bloating in her stomach. She slapped a package of red licorice down on the counter. The two little boys lined up behind her.

"Get laid last night, Forehead?"

"Did you?" he said, the words squashed and limp.

"At least I do it with the opposite sex."

His face went red like a baby's when it tries to go to the bathroom, and she had to hold herself back from slapping it, making it redder, making it sting.

"You're mean," one of the little boys said. She turned, and he was looking at her fiercely, his eyes almost lost in his freckles. He kicked her, and then, seeming to like the feeling, punched her breast. "I could kill you," he said. "I know how."

"Right," Sandra said, and she went outside, not bothering with the licorice, trying not to cry from the pain, wiping at her eyes. She wanted to touch her breast to make it feel better, but she didn't. She first stood by the garbage can, full of pop cans and chocolate bar wrappers and popsicle sticks, but a wasp dove at her ear, so she stood by the fence, leaned against it. She had a flash—she often had flashes—of her father, straightening a pile of paper at work.

The boys came out like they'd won something. They grabbed their bikes that leaned against the front of the store. They didn't hurry at all.

"Think you're big, don't you?" the little boy who had hit her said. His voice shook like a girl's, and he was blushing. His friend concentrated on his ketchup chips, his eyes narrow and unafraid.

"Fuck off," she said.

"Ooh, I'm scared," he said, and got on his bike and, nosing the front wheel at her legs, ran over her foot. She grabbed the handles to stop him as a man walked up with his Lab, and the boy whispered to Sandra, "I'm going to kill you. I'm going to dig your grave tonight."

Her chin trembled, but the man came closer to them and the boys sped away, the one with freckles laughing in his throat, as if meeting Sandra had given him a million good ideas.

Ingrid appeared with her Fun Dip and they made their way to Tom's. A light wind from the lake floated through the trees and down the street. The sun was fully out now, warming the top of Sandra's head.

When they got to his three-storey house, Ingrid knocked and, after a minute, Tom answered in black jeans, a white shirt tucked in. He had black hair that winged out at his ears, one of which was pierced with a gold stud. He smelled of soap and sweet chemicals. Classical music played in the house.

"Hey, Queen Bee."

"Can we come in?" Ingrid asked.

Sandra could tell that Ingrid's body had started humming—her skin became a deeper pink, and one bird hand fluttered up to her temple, then fell to her side.

"*Entrez*," Tom said, and Ingrid's shoulders came together as she stepped in. Her giggle sounded like a gag. One ribbon dangled from her hair and her eyes squinted as if they suddenly stung. She dug into her bottom lip with her top teeth.

"Come upstairs. Tell her to go home," Tom said, motioning toward Sandra. Ingrid's red lips opened, and now her eyes widened. She turned to Sandra.

"Go home. I'll phone you," Ingrid said, and walked up the stairs without waiting for a reply.

Outside, Sandra felt temporarily free. She took off her rain coat and carried it.

The air reeked of grass and flowers. She walked along the shoulder of the road toward the lake. The lake was hers. It had always been hers. It was rough today, a vicious beast. When she was eight and nine, she'd swum in it bravely, done somersaults and handstands, lashed out to the sandbar. Today, even though the sun poured down, the water discouraged her. The mouths of waves choked up foam, and she had the feeling she always had that she was ugly, a pulsing blob of flesh—she didn't want to die, but hated to be a living thing. She headed away from the lake along a path that ran beside the field. It was empty and quiet during the day. At night, when there were boys there, things could happen, things a girl wanted to happen. The ones who wanted it never ran fast enough. She was going to have to go there, and she was going to have let them, and it couldn't wait. She needed to be altered.

The house was empty and quiet when she got home because her mother went to the gym in the afternoons. Stiff and wary in the silence, Sandra set her key on the front table. The hush of the house always invited Sandra to do the thing she didn't want to but had to do. She climbed the stairs, excited and full of dread. She walked to the end of the hall and entered her parents' bedroom. A school picture of her brother sat on their dresser, and Sandra glanced at it briefly and guiltily. She slid her mother's mirrored closet door closed and glanced at her watch. Then she pushed down her jeans, pulled her top over her head, unclipped her bra. Laying on her back on her mother's side of the bed, Sandra glanced at herself in the mirror. Her face was spotty and despicable. She closed her eyes and raised her hands above her head—she was out of control now, and hated herself, could taste the hate like onions in her mouth, and she wasn't going to let herself have Oreos after. Sandra kept her hands above her head, imagining what she had to imagine, that she was helpless, tied up. A line up of boys from her class stood outside the room, and they were determined, and Sandra was their slave—an ache in her body, a deep down thrumming. Then she hurriedly went down the hall to her own room, put the pillow between her legs, and she finished—melted warmly all over it.

The day had become an even hotter one, and when Sandra's mother came home from the gym, she cranked the air-conditioning. Sandra wore socks and jeans and a sweater as she lay on the couch watching General Hospital. Her mother was upset with her because she had called home to tell Sandra to take chicken out of the freezer, and Sandra hadn't been home. Now Sandra was saying that she hadn't heard the phone because she was sleeping, but her mother didn't believe that for a minute; she said she could tell by Sandra's eyes that she was lying.

"And get off that couch. Lying like that is terrible for your posture."

At first, Sandra said nothing, then she said, "Leave me alone."

Her mother stood in front of the television.

"Get up."

"No."

"Yes."

She rolled over to her other side and buried her face in the upholstery, a comforting, long-ago smell.

"Sandra, what is wrong with you?"

She was comforted by the sound of her own breathing, could almost block her mother out, go into her own, lovely, quiet world.

A claw on her shoulder. "Get up. I want the lawn mowed before your father gets back."

"Cunt," Sandra said. "Fucking stupid cunt." She had said it before, but only in her head. She liked the way the words sounded together, like rocks being thrown at something, killing it.

Her mother whipped her around and smacked her jaw so hard that her molars hurt. Her mother's eyes were full of dislike and bitterness. She wished that her mother could have been more attractive, for her own sake. Her silk blouses didn't soften her or make her prettier. Her eyelashes were long and dark with mascara, her lids dull brown with shadow, but the eyes were full of contempt. She knew her mother wished it had been Sandra and not her brother.

"I'll do it, just leave me alone."

"You better," her mother said. In a moment, Sandra heard footsteps going down the basement stairs.

Early in the evening, Sandra drove with her father to pick up the pizza they'd ordered. Her father was so tall that he had had to duck and fold himself into the blue Mustang.

It was the end of summer. Dusk fell all around them, and even though it was warm, Sandra felt a deep chill, as if water had pooled inside of her.

She drove with him whenever it was possible because she worried about her father. Sandra worried that he would die in a car crash, and something that she wanted to say to him—she didn't know what exactly—would be forever unsaid. She believed her presence would prevent the accident. Metal crashing into metal, blood pouring out, her father's face stony and satisfied, pleased at his unexpected escape.

Sandra kept glancing at him, trying to think of what she wanted to say. His hair was grey, and he was thin and, since her brother had died, he didn't like to talk. He sometimes spoke to the newspaper, which he read when he got home from work, a glass of stinging whiskey in his hand. If Sandra needed to speak to him at all, it was important she did it early in the evening. After a certain time, a few hours after he got home, her father's face became more and more open, and his eyes looked different—bigger, glassy, leaking desperation. Sometimes, when he was like this, her father would want Sandra to sit beside him, not talk, but just sit beside him, and he liked to put his long arm around her. He'd tell her how much he loved her and he'd ask her to say it back, but because of the smell of his breath, none of what he said went in. All of it exhausted her, made her squeamish and depressed. Soon he'd fall asleep, snoring and gasping, and she'd creep away. Her mother was always trying to live in another world, a world that was muted, where nothing happened, and she could live in her own thoughts and not be disturbed. On Saturdays, her mother would sit on the end of the couch with one of her thrillers, her thin, long, brown hair hanging straight down to her shoulders. After she finished the book, she'd lie on the couch with her hands pressed together like leaves under her cheek. In the house on Saturdays, Sandra sometimes felt like an abomination, too alive.

"I can't wait to eat," Sandra said, putting her hand on her stomach.

"Yes," her father said, and she wasn't sure if he was responding to what she had said or if he was answering a thought.

He parked outside of Pizza Hut, pulled the gearshift back.

She stayed in her seat while her father went in. He walked on a slant, how rain fell. The heavy door closed behind him. He had left the radio on for her and she turned the knob, trying to find "Every Breath You Take." No station was playing it.

After a few minutes, her father emerged from the restaurant with a pizza box in his hands. He opened the car door.

"Hi," she said, but he said nothing, just nodded and handed her the pizza. He started the car, reversed, turned toward the exit, and it was on the tip of her tongue—the boys at the store. Maybe she would even tell him they had had a knife. They drove across the bridge, then along the long, curving road that bordered the marsh before turning into their little neighbourhood on the edge of the lake. Sandra wanted to stay in the car with her father, even though they seldom spoke. She wanted the car to keep moving, she wanted to be perpetually in motion—it would save her from something, she wasn't sure what. The creeping chill she had felt earlier simply made her anxious; the leaves flipping and turning in the wind that had come up off the lake filled her with a strange, tense worry about herself. She was a small figure in the world, and nothing was attached to her, and she was not attached to anything. Her skin hurt, and suddenly she felt dizzy.

Sandra glanced at her father. He smiled at something in his head— it couldn't have been at the thought of her, or the thought of her mother. He couldn't have been thinking about her brother, either.

She looked ahead. The lake lay before her; it would always be hers. But she wasn't going to be able to tell him; he might not have said anything. He might have told her none of it sounded likely, or that she'd be fine, they were just little boys. Before, when he had picked her up from a basketball tournament in Oshawa, she'd told him about the boys in the field, how they held girls down and the girls didn't struggle, how they laughed and liked it, and he had peered at her, peered at her as if he could see her, and he had said, "That sounds awful. That doesn't sound like something you want to have happen to you." For weeks, she had played that over in her head, his voice and how he had looked at her, absorbing her; she could feel herself being almost physically absorbed by him. For those weeks, it wasn't something Sandra had wanted to have happen to her. She had been pure. She had been in control.

Sandra led the way. At night, the field was a different place: it was neutral. It inhaled and exhaled without feeling. Sandra and Ingrid had snuck out. Sandra phoned her after pizza and they made the plan. It had been easy, and she had done it once before. She quietly and slowly opened the bedroom door, quietly and slowly went down the front stairs, then squeezed herself out the front door. She didn't bother bunching clothes up under her blanket. No one would look, she was sure. The last time she'd gone out with Ingrid, they couldn't find anything to do, and Sandra had been grumpy and cold, not realizing how much the temperature dropped at night and how wet and chilly the grass was. They had trampled a couple of gardens, broken one antenna. They hadn't even talked about going to the field, and had finally parted on the corner they always parted on. Sandra had run home, and she had felt like an animal, hearing her jagged, harsh breath in her ears, feeling ropy and fierce. She had kept looking behind her.

But tonight, she had a purpose.

The field breathed, and Sandra fiddled with a loose thread in the pocket of her green jacket. There was a hole in the pocket, and she could stick her hand right through it. She did that now, and found a small pencil. She held it in her hand, squeezed it. It was the one she chewed on in school; her mouth often tasted like pencil wood.

Sandra and Ingrid sat across from each other in the pit, a dirt hollow surrounded by skinny, leafy trees and bushes. Sandra sat on a piece of board, and Ingrid sat on an IGA supermarket bag that she had brought with her. "He popped my cherry," Ingrid had said earlier, smiling, but with a tense mouth. From where Sandra was sitting, she could see a portion of the street; she saw two boys walk under the street lamp. They had long hair and wore jean jackets— both of them. They were older boys who were in high school. They might have known her brother. One might have said, "We miss that guy." The boys vanished.

Every time Ingrid puffed on her cigarette, her long nose and wide eyes were narrowly lit up.

"Why are we here again?" she said.

"I want to see what it's like at night."

"You know what happens here," Ingrid said, and she tapped ash off her cigarette, as if she were now ten years older than Sandra.

"So. We're fine."

"My ass is getting cold."

"Ten more minutes."

Ingrid got up. "I'm getting the hell out of here." She stood in a way that was artificial, like a grown woman talking to a child.

"Ten more minutes."

"You want them to," Ingrid said. "You're so gross."

"Want them to do what?" Sandra asked, and she felt her chest freeze.

"I just think it's disturbing," Ingrid said, using a tone she'd never used before, and Sandra wondered where she'd heard it. "And I'm probably the one they'd chase anyway." She smiled at Sandra, and Sandra imagined what it would have been like with Tom; had Ingrid taken all of her clothes off.

"Sorry." She got up.

Sandra watched her progress across the field. She had small, bony shoulders, long, thin arms. She had told Sandra before that the only thing she didn't like about her body was her feet. Ingrid stepped onto the road and headed home, and the tall bushes on the side of the road concealed her.

Sandra was alone. She tried to stay still on the board and to breathe through her fear. She looked at her white running shoes, then at her hands on her thighs. She had that dizzy sensation again. Whose hands were those? Whose legs and feet were those? Then the field was sucking her in, folding her up; it wanted her, and would get her. She got up automatically, something from deep inside pushed her up, and she started running.

That night, when Sandra opened the front door, her mother appeared in the kitchen doorway with a mug of coffee in her hand, her narrow, flabby face wretched with exhaustion and worry. She was wearing her rose velour robe, tied up tightly at the waist, and the pink collar of her pyjamas was sticking out.

"Where were you?"

"Out," Sandra said. She hung up her coat in the closet. She took out the small pencil and put it in the front pocket of her jeans.

"Don't be flippant with me. And what's in your pocket?"

Sandra held out the small, bitten pencil, then put it back in her pocket. "I was out. With Ingrid. What am I supposed to say?"

"Don't you know that I worry about you?"

Sandra walked to the foot of the stairs. She stopped. "Don't think I don't know the truth." She climbed up the stairs to her bedroom. Below, her mother whispered, "What truth?" but Sandra closed her bedroom door. If her mother really knew what the truth was, she wouldn't knock. If Sandra was wrong, if she was all wrong and her mother really couldn't live without her, she would knock, wanting to know what Sandra thought the truth was.

It wasn't his room at all anymore. And no one would ever have known what he had done in this room. Still, when Ingrid came over, she wouldn't step across the threshold.

It had all the possible comforts: a down comforter, a frilly bed-skirt, pillows, stuffed animals, a desk, plush blue carpet, a closet full of dresses, like a doll's closet. Before her brother died, her mother had bought her a dress for every season; after, dresses didn't seem important anymore, didn't seem like something Sandra should ask for. Now, she liked jeans and sweaters and running shoes.

When she had said she wanted her brother's old room, her father had gone to the trouble of fixing it up for her, and even though it was so long ago, it was how she knew he loved her, really loved her. She changed into her yellow nightgown, got under the covers, lay straight out on her back. She liked to feel that her comforter was hugging her. Her blind was up, and from this position she could see the top floor of the neighbour's house, the sky beyond, and she felt afraid and excited; afraid because the world had no end and excited because she was alive, her blood was moving, and she was Sandra, and no one else was. It was her night feeling; it came at night when she was alone in her bedroom, and the next day, she could only remember the feeling. She took a deep, deep breath, held it for as long as she could, then let it out, a warm stream passing out her mouth.

She closed her eyes, held herself tightly.

Below this room was the living room where she and her brother used to fight, wrestling and attacking each other. He had been three years older, and he could have really hurt Sandra, but he never did. Her body would knock against his, his body would knock against hers—and that was what she had wanted. He pinned her, and she pinned him, holding his warm sweaty hands against the carpet, threatening to spit in his face. Sometimes she kissed him hard and wet on the forehead, pretending it was the worst punishment of all. He smelled like smoke, and sometimes his eyes were red and swollen. After, he'd get up, straighten himself out, and say, "Okay, now leave me alone the rest of the night." She would. Didn't he know she had been completely satisfied? She let him close himself up in his room.

Everyone thought it was the pot. That he had killed himself because his friend's dad caught him selling drugs outside the store while Sandra and her mother and father were at the cottage for the weekend. Sandra had swum and roasted marshmallows and played cards with her mother and tanned with her on a rock they'd swum out to in the afternoon. Her father had taken her out waterskiing, and Sandra had gotten up on the first try. She had risen up, miraculously, and she had not fallen. She couldn't stop smiling, and wind had blown her teeth, gums, and tongue dry. Her father had boasted to everyone, and her mother kept saying she must have waterskiing legs.

Her brother had been home, and he'd been caught selling pot. Still, Sandra thought it was something else: his nighttime feeling had been different, scarier; it had been hollow and unbearable. She hadn't been there to hug him and soothe him.

She sat up in bed, trying to imagine the hollowness, the not caring if you lived or if you died, wanting to die. She closed her eyes; she wanted to feel herself disappearing, giving up. She lay back down and opened her eyes. What came to her mind then was the hardness and warmth of his forehead against her lips. Her hands, small in his.

She pulled her comforter up to her chin. Odd thoughts wandered into her mind at night. Sometimes she wanted to know how she was supposed to know that she was supposed to be alive. But tonight she looked out, and it came to her: because I'm not dead.

She heard her mother gently climb the stairs, one step at a time, slowly, so they creaked and groaned; then she passed Sandra's bedroom door as if she hadn't seen it in the dark.

Embrace

I CROSSED AVENUE ROAD, my face tilted up at the light snow that fell. Some movement caught my eye, and I turned toward it. An old man was opening his arms to me. His jacket flapped, his pants ended above his ankles, and he walked as if he would tip forward as he enfolded me. He looked lost, and I was afraid. I knew right away that I had been mistaken for someone else, or that I struck him as compassionate, someone who would return his embrace. He reached for me, and I trudged past him.

By the time I reached the outside of my grey walk-up, the tips of my fingers were red and numb.

Last night, Scott had told me that it had never been more than us having sex, and that I had tried to trap him, but that it hadn't worked. I had suffered for that, and the suffering had been my choice.

My apartment was like an aquarium, and I was the lone fish swimming through it. I floated down the hall toward the bedroom; my unfolded laundry was in a pile on my bed. When I picked it up and carried it over to the dresser, I liked the feeling of it in my arms. If I left the blinds open, I could see into the apartment across from mine. A fat woman my age, maybe a bit younger, lived there, and every time I looked, she was lying on her couch with her feet up on the end, watching television. Usually, there was a blue light flickering over her, except when the scene was dark; then, she was in sombre shadows. Sometimes I wondered if she ever saw me and what she thought of me if she did.

I phoned Reg. He was forty-two and a carpenter, and I had seen him once, a few weeks after I'd gone to the clinic and lost what I'd lost. But then I put an end to it, and now I liked being his friend. He answered on the second ring.

"Want to come over?" I asked, sitting on the edge of my bed.

"I'm in the middle of laundry," he said.

"I want to go out," I said. "I don't have any money, though. I could pay you back."

"Don't worry about it."

After we hung up, I cleaned the apartment, changed the sheets on my bed. Then I buttoned up a white blouse to go with my black skirt. At the window, I watched the snow fall. I was excited, as if my veins were crawling with frenzied spiders. I wanted to want him.

I had met him on the subway. I was on my way home from the flower shop and he was standing above me, holding onto the pole, steadying himself, and he asked me what I thought of the book I was reading, *Les Misérables*. I had only been staring at the words, unable to concentrate, but I told him I liked it. I had bought it on my lunch; I had liked the title and heaviness, and I thought it might make me smarter, make me someone who knew things. Reg got off the subway with me, and I liked even more having the weight and height of a man next to me, lending me something, and I went for beer with him. He had small, sharp blue eyes, a plump mouth, and black hair that was grey at the sides. He looked strong, and I could imagine him carrying a canoe over his head. When he kissed me that night, his eyes got anxious, as if he were watching me get sucked away by a black wind.

Reg came up the walk. I let him in, my voice falsely gleeful over the intercom. In a minute, he was banging on the door.

I opened it, wanting to see his face, how happy he was to see me.

His ears and nose were red, and his small blue eyes watered as if they had been poked. Seeing him, I wanted to lean into him and smell his leather jacket; I would like the smell.

"For you," he said, offering a white bag.

"Me?"

"Couldn't resist," he said.

He told me he bought it a week ago in the Eaton Centre.

In the hall mirror, Reg brushed dissolving snow from his hair with his gloves. Out of the bag I pulled a green wool coat with a hood. Once I had it on, Reg leaned in and kissed my neck, and I stiffened. He smelled cold, like snow on ice at nighttime, and faintly, dizzyingly sweet.

"You can throw out that other one," he said. "When I first saw you in it, I thought, get that girl a coat." He laughed a salty laugh and his body curled in—I didn't like his laugh. Buttoned up in this new, green wool coat, though, I felt young. I felt like someone who should be taken care of. People would see me on the street holding hands with Reg, and they would think that I was happy, that there was nothing wrong with me.

"I want to go out," I said.

"I don't blame you," he said. "Now that you have something half-decent to put on."

Then he said, "Do you have a scarf?"

"It doesn't match."

"Here, wear mine."

"It doesn't match, either. You need it. I'm not going to take your scarf." And I wanted, again, to lean into him. I resisted.

"You look cute," Reg said, and he curled a long, dark bang behind my ear. He held my face in his hands, and I kept my head very still. Up close, his eyes were blue dimes with black cracks; little mountainous lines radiated out from the pupils.

"Thank you," I said.

Outside, we walked for several blocks through a blowing fall of icy snow.

Reg grabbed my hand. "You're not wearing gloves," he said. "What's wrong with you?" His hand was wide and gripped mine so hard, I couldn't move my fingers.

"I want you to wear my scarf," he said again. We stopped outside a bright dollar store—snow had begun to gather on sand pails and umbrellas. He removed his scarf, a man's scarf, striped grey and burgundy. When we'd met on the subway, he was wearing it, and it had been a beacon of some sort, something from my past, something from far away.

"No," I said, and helped him to wind it back up.

He led us to a diner with orange booths and metal lamps that hung over the tables. In the back, where it must have been warm, a couple sat with their small boy. His hair stood up in thin curls, and I wanted to run my hand across them, feel the temperature of his head with my closed lips.

Before we sat down, Reg brushed snow from my hair, and I liked that feeling. I brushed snow from his hair. People would assume we were in love.

We sat across from each other in a booth by the window.

"You're not going to take your coat off?"

I shook my head, then held my hand up to the window. "Draft," I said. But then I unbuttoned it.

"You do look beautiful in it."

"Thanks," I said.

"You know, you're really very beautiful."

I smiled.

"That wasn't real."

"It was."

"I don't understand you," he said. "You're a weird girl." He peered out the window, exhaled heavily. Then he leaned forward and rested his arms on the table, as if he didn't want to go anywhere.

"I really want you to meet my son," he said. "I was thinking about it." Reg had had two sons, but one had died in a car accident—his car slid off an icy road and slammed into a pole—when he was sixteen.

"I'd like to."

"Good kid. Mixed up right now. I'd like to wait."

"I'd like to, though," I said, because I didn't want to forget the possibility of us. One day, I might have leaned into him and allowed myself to be held. "You're probably a good father."

The waitress arrived—an old woman with harsh blonde hair; it would have been rough against my palm. She stood and smiled with her small, white notepad; as if there was something wrong with me, as if I deserved her pity and not the other way around. I ordered a hamburger and french fries and a Coke, and Reg ordered roast beef. The waitress shuffled away.

"So, you'd like to meet him?"

I nodded, peering out the window again. I had to figure things out, so I didn't become old and poor, a woman who could be thrown aside, sexless and ugly, shuffling in bright diners late at night, serving Reg and me.

"It'll be good," Reg said. His eyes were wide, and he had that look, as if I were blowing away in the wind and he was helpless.

"It will be," I said.

In the glass, I could see the waitress shuffle to another booth where two men, both with shaved heads, sat across from each other.

"What are you thinking right now?" Reg asked. "You must be thinking something."

"I am," I said. I brought my hands together, rested my chin on them.

"You're probably thinking you don't want to have anything to do with me. Am I right?"

I shook my head.

"Then what?"

"I was just thinking—I would hate to be old."

"Everyone gets old."

"Well, I don't want to."

"The alternative is to die young."

"I don't want that either."

The waitress trundled into the back, and I leaned in and whispered, "I don't want to be like her."

Reg smiled, leaned back, squinted. "You? You could never be like that."

"I might be," I said. "If things don't change." Then I said, "That's why I have to make them change."

"What do you want to change?"

"It doesn't matter."

"It doesn't matter?"

I shook my head.

Reg tapped his fingers and regarded me as if he wanted to say something but might have been afraid to say it. "Maybe you'll find some rich guy," he said.

"That's not what I'm talking about."

In a minute, the waitress brought our food, and I avoided her eyes.

In the back, the young woman bundled up her son in a blue hat and a red coat. He would be warm; no wind would penetrate to disturb his comfort.

"You're not going to eat?" Reg said.

He forked a big piece of roast beef, dripping with gravy, into his mouth. I was in the wrong place with the wrong person. But I would have been lonelier without him, a young woman no one would have to respect, pay attention to.

"Eat," he said.

"He's sixteen this month," Reg said. "Typical boy. Takes off in the middle of class. Wanders around the neighbourhood. She found him asleep one night in the park. Stretched out on a picnic table."

I looked out the window. A man holding a bouquet of flowers walked past.

"I think we should forget this," Reg said.

"Forget what?"

"You, me. You're always somewhere else. Time to move on."

"I'm sorry," I said.

"Don't be."

"We should go, then."

He got the waitress's attention, then held his hand in the air and signed an imaginary cheque. Pieces of roast beef and shiny carrots and potatoes were left on his plate, and they suddenly looked good.

I buttoned up my coat, thinking it would bring me a shiver of pleasure, hoping it would. The coat was the beginning of things changing.

The waitress brought the bill. I refused to look at her. I wished she would die. After Reg paid, we got up to go.

He held the door open, and I marched through. He boomed goodnight to the waitress, and she called goodnight back.

"I'll walk you home," he said.

"No."

"What? You're not through with me yet?"

"Maybe I want a drink."

"Do you or don't you?"

"I do."

I couldn't explain, but I needed Reg. I couldn't toss him overboard. We got to an intersection, and we crossed on a red because there were hardly any cars out. The falling snow was the kind I remembered as a child, falling on the bare apple tree in our front yard, laying itself on the branches. I would open my mouth and taste it, catch flakes on my blue woollen mittens. I could never have imagined then how I felt now, that the world was folding up and that I was not in it.

Reg grabbed my hand again—this time with such force that I was overwhelmed. Wind and snow pushed against my bare neck, and I scrunched my shoulders up, ducked to protect myself. When we reached the other side, Reg stopped me, took control. He unwound his scarf and wrapped it three times around my neck, covering my mouth and nose with it, knotting it at the front so it would stay in place. "I don't give a fuck if it doesn't match," he said.

"Where are we going?" I asked, tasting wool. My breath created a warm, wet spot, and my voice was muffled.

"You'll see," he said, and I liked that, him leading the way, so I didn't have to think.

While we walked, the snow lashed at my eyes, and something dark and noxious slid out of me, and hope slid in. I felt sure that if I wanted Reg, I could become the woman he wanted forever. I liked having the scarf wrapped around my neck, tied up securely at the front, shielding my nose and mouth. The people who passed us would think I lived in a house, that I took good care of a child, that I was light and clear and steadfast. I liked that Reg had tied the scarf, and I wished that others had seen him do it, seen me standing there with my hands in my pockets as he tied it. Reg was a good man. I could marry him and have a child. My heart pounded.

"I wish I had eaten."

"You're a typical woman."

He stopped. He pulled open the door of a dark pub that was almost empty.

There was a fire in the corner.

"I want to sit with my back to it," I said.

"Demanding," Reg said. "You're the captain of the ship."

We sat near the fire in white chairs that were meant to be plush and luxurious and comfortable but were dingy and stiff. I unwound the scarf, and this time I shouldered the coat off and rested it on my lap.

Reg rested his hands on the table, tapped the fingers of one. I took his hands in mine.

"Hairy fingers," I said.

"You think so?"

"I like them," I said. "And I know I like you."

"I had a wife that liked to dick me around."

I stroked the black hair above his knuckles. "I'm not going to do that."

"I wouldn't expect you to admit it if you were going to. That's not usually how it works." He laughed through his nose, but he allowed me to continue stroking the hair on his hands. He watched my fingers.

"I just know I'm not going to," I said. "You're mature."

"So if I was younger, you would?"

I shrugged and let go of his hands. The heat of the fire lunged up my back, and my neck started sweating.

"You'll see," I said.

"You're just so passionless," he said. "I've never met anyone so passionless."

An old Italian man came to take our order. He grinned at me as though, for some reason, he was immensely impressed with me.

I ordered a Guinness and Reg ordered chicken fingers and a Heineken.

Before he left, the waiter winked at me, and I wondered what he saw.

"I'm sorry," Reg said.

"I just don't see how I am."

"Forget it. I didn't mean it."

"I know I'm tired all the time. And that I need money."

Reg reached out and touched my arm. "I like this blouse," he said. "I like how soft it is. I can see right through it." He rubbed my arm and looked at me, and his face fell, and his eyes were warm, pressing against mine. I looked away. I looked away without meaning to look away. Then he stroked my fingers. I liked it, the attention he gave my fingers. In his hands, my fingers belonged to someone who didn't have to worry. Reg leaned across the table to kiss me, and I leaned into him, trying it. His lips were soft and wet and chilly. He smelled like ice. We pulled apart.

"I was just thinking I could be a legal secretary. They make more money than regular secretaries, I think."

"Why don't you?"

"I might," I said, and wiped sweat from the back of my neck.

"You worry too much." He touched the arm of my blouse again, rubbed his hand up and down, and I shivered.

Later, the snow kept falling. Reg made me wear his scarf again. We bumped into each other as we walked. Snow gathered in his hair, a frail, glittering net. I should have hungered for him. He was a muscular man, and he believed women were fragile. A group of girls spilled out of a bar, laughing at something. One girl in a black skirt and bare legs slipped and fell in the snow; her laughter was a low, hysterical vibration from her body. Reg could have helped her up, taken her home, and she could have devoured him. After we passed the girls, I brushed his cheek with my fingers. He took my hand and I became filled with a strange, radiant belief in myself. I would not die old and alone. I was not like the waitress. I was not wrinkled and ugly and over. With Reg, things would work out, and my other longings would go away.

"How are you?" he asked. Snow was hitting his face and neck, but he looked at me with concern, as if, if I were not okay, he would do something about it.

"Fine."

He smiled at that. He smiled at me as if I were peculiar but probably couldn't help it, as if I might be harmless.

He squeezed my hand so I couldn't wiggle my fingers. And I was going to love Reg because he could love me. I was going to make myself do it. I would not grieve. I opened my mouth to the snow, barely visible in the dark air above me, and let it melt on my tongue.

In the Midnight Cold

SARA AND IAN SAT at the dining room table, and snow was falling outside. They were having their glass of red wine, as they did every night when Ian first arrived home. Ian's job was stressful. He was a structural engineer, and he had deadlines, people counting on him. Sara taught ESL, whenever she could get the work. This winter, she was off. At six o'clock, half an hour earlier, when Ian called to say he was finally on his way, she set two wine glasses and the bottle of red on the table, lit the white candles.

"What do you want for dinner?" Ian said.

"I want to go out," she said. She rubbed her arms because the room was chilly.

"Sure."

"It's Friday night, anyway," Sara said. She always looked forward to Friday nights because Ian was relaxed, and his eyes rested on her more, as if he were wondering how she was feeling.

"True." Ian picked up his glass and took a sip. He had short, grey hair and large, almost feminine blue eyes, and a beard he kept very trim—he was nine years older than Sara. When they first met, she was drawn to his beard, black then. It made him seem masculine, like someone who would always be in control, who would always know the answers.

"What did you do today?" Ian said.

"I took Brittany to Riverdale," she said. "She was biting the leash. I called you, but you didn't answer."

"Why did you call me? Because she was biting the leash?"

"I didn't know what to do."

He studied her, two fingers on the stem of his glass. "What did you think I was going to do?"

She stood, walked over to the thermostat, and turned up the heat from twenty-one, where Ian insisted it stay, to twenty-five. Then she sat down and looked out at the patio. The candle flames reflected in the glass. Sometimes Sara thought it was the winter they were having—long and wet and cold—that explained why she bristled at Ian. Winters were always cold, but different in the way they were cold and the way in which the cold disrupted life. This winter, the sky was grey for weeks, and sudden warm days produced rain that cold days then froze. The sidewalks were often icy, forcing Sara, when she went to the grocery store or to Riverdale Park, to walk more slowly, as if she were mildly disabled.

"Do you feel like Greek?" he asked.

"Okay," Sara said, even though she didn't. Greek food was for the summer.

But she was hungry, and her stomach was tight. Whenever she grew aware of her stomach, she remembered Joanne. The first time Joanne went to the doctor this past spring, they ran tests, and the doctors told her nothing was wrong. Joanne and her husband went out to dinner to celebrate the news, but then two days later the doctor called and asked her to come back in. He told Joanne she had cancer in her stomach and that she would not live. She was buried in the early autumn, when the leaves were reddening but not yet detaching. Sara and Joanne had met in university. They were supposed to grow old together.

"I'm going to take Brittany out," Sara said.

The moment she heard her name, the black, furry, snoozing heap that was Brittany put all four legs into scrambling action.

Sara came back inside with Brittany. The shower was running upstairs. Sara unclipped the dog's leash, let her run up to the third floor to lie outside the bathroom, then refilled her wine glass. She'd learned over the years that Ian was someone who liked to shower alone—she'd tried to cure him of this, but after a while, she could no longer stand the rejection. Ian said not wanting to shower with her wasn't rejection, it had nothing to do with not being attracted to her—he needed to think through problems in the shower. If he didn't get things right, structures failed, people possibly died, and money was lost. He was liable for the rest of his life. He didn't want to be in the news, he said.

Sara sat in the living room, sipping her wine. These past months, since not renewing her teaching contract, she had almost lived in this room. The window looked down onto the garden, where the ivy was still alive. Three bookshelves leaned against each other, and the lamps attempted to glow. After ten years together, Sara and Ian had collected three lamps. One had belonged to Ian's mother. The shade was pink and pleated, like his mother's personality, the personality that helped shape Ian into the precise person he was. The other was a green, antique metal reading lamp that Sara had asked for, for her birthday, which Ian hated but bought anyway. He did almost everything she asked. The third was a lamp with a modern white, cylindrical shade that was purchased to lend light, not because either of them liked it.

On the wall beside the window hung a photograph of Brittany with her feet in Lake Huron. Without shame, Ian and Sara thought of Brittany as their beastly, exquisitely loyal child. In the picture, Brittany glared at the camera.

Sara remembered that day—the long drive, all the things she'd said to Ian, and how he'd listened. Whenever they went on long car trips, he listened and talked more than he did at home. Maybe he felt free, like a man not an engineer, a slave to his calculations, projects, clients. At home, he always seemed to be having a conversation with someone else in his head. His lips even moved. At least a couple of times a week he talked in his sleep, waking Sara, but it wasn't really talking—he spit out numbers. Some nights, he sat at the computer like a man at the helm of a ship, alert, ready. On this particular ride to Lake Huron, because he didn't like listening to the radio, Sara's voice became the constant music. Sara told the stories from her youth: how she smoked pot every day after school, blasting her eardrums with Judas Priest, and how she sat at the dinner table stoned, pressing her fork onto her mound of mashed potatoes. Her mother, absorbed in her own thoughts, never noticed. A year later, when Sara lived with her father, she failed every subject at school, but her father never knew because he was busy running around his house, away from the flying fists of his new wife. Sara once climbed into the trunk of a car full of boys and let them drive her to the beach. She told Ian the same stories over and over, as if she could not comprehend them; she needed them out of her, and into Ian. Ian always said, "You were a wild child, that's for sure." What he said made her feel that some order had been brought to the situation, some calm.

Sara went down to the kitchen—each room was on a different floor—to make herself toast. Ian didn't snack because his mother had forbidden him to eat between meals, so when Sara snacked, she tried to gobble things up secretly, so Ian wouldn't say, "You're going to spoil your dinner." Sara's mother had never said those words. Sara ate whenever she wanted to eat. There was always more room, a pocket of space.

The toast popped and Sara buttered it. If she chewed quickly and washed it down with her wine (she ate combinations that revolted Ian), he would never know. Sara watched the butter melt into the toast. She carried the plate upstairs, sat on the couch, and took small bites of the toast, sucking the butter, letting the bread dissolve on her tongue.

"What are you eating?" Ian said. He stood naked and dry at the top of the stairs. His penis eyed her.

"What does it look like?"

"You're going to spoil your dinner."

"I guess that's my business."

Ian sighed, muttered something, then climbed the stairs to the bedroom. Brittany toddled downstairs to Sara instead of following Ian upstairs. She sat panting gently, her soft ears flat. Her eyes were enlarged, a brown that sparkled.

Brittany laid a paw on Sara's leg, smiling in the way dogs do. Slanted eyes, the lips curled. Sara didn't know if it was a smile or not.

"No toast, honey," Sara said. She lifted Brittany's paw off her leg. Brittany sat looking at Sara for a second, then ran upstairs to the bedroom where Ian was. Ian never believed what Brittany was capable of understanding.

He came downstairs a few minutes later. Brittany would be on her back on the bed. Ian smelled of the soap that only he was allowed to use. It had a medicinal smell, but the scent faded so that at night she could only detect it if she put her face in his neck, after sex. She liked the smell, and she liked the sex, the feel of him inside her, the way he pulled at her, even bit and slapped her. He was wearing jeans and a white shirt with blue lines on it. All of his shirts were variations on the theme of blue-and-white lines.

Sara sipped her wine, then took a bite of her toast.

Ian sat on the chair on the other side of the coffee table, like a father on television about to lecture his teenage daughter. He tilted his head to the side, his eyes generous and indulgent, as if readying himself for her lame excuses. Behind him leaned the bookshelves— his books and her books. Ian read history and architecture. He had wanted to be an architect, but there was no money in it. Sara read fiction and poetry and plays. The television was a lifeless decoration, something Sara thought they were supposed to have to make the room complete.

"How are you doing?" Ian said.

"It's time for dinner," Sara said. "I'm hungry. You were late coming home."

"What are you implying?"

"That you were late coming home."

"I need to work, Sara. People are counting on me. What am I supposed to do when someone drops a pile of work on my desk?"

Sara studied her fingernails. She'd filed and polished them this afternoon, but the pink she'd chosen wasn't hot enough. Since Joanne died, she needed colour.

She went upstairs to the bathroom. The small space smelled mildewy because of all the rain. The walls needed painting. Ian promised to fix things, but he didn't have time. He came in after her. She was brushing on her steel-blue eye shadow.

The bathroom was too bright because of the three halogen light bulbs in the fixture above the sink. The lights had been there when they moved in. Sara hated the room.

Ian asked, "Why are you so tense all the time?"

The floor was still wet from his shower. No matter his usual precision, he never wiped up after himself. She stepped in puddles. She glanced at her wedding ring in the mirror: the white-gold band needed polishing. She stretched the fingers out on her hand.

"Tell me," he said so quietly it was as if he thought someone else might overhear him.

Sara set the applicator in its case and clicked it shut. She put it back in the medicine cabinet where Ian insisted it go. Everything had a place, he always said.

She looked at her eyes, checking for evenness, then stuck a finger in her lip gloss and smoothed it on, pinking her lips. Sara pushed past him to escape the bathroom. She descended the stairs. The question was always this: would he follow her? He was following her. She loved that feeling—it dispersed all anxiety, fear, dread, pain. When he caught up to her, he might hold her.

Their front entrance was too small, and they always banged elbows and arms when they put on their scarves, hats, and gloves. They got ready, and Sara did not meet his eyes. Then they performed their ritual. Ian checked Sara's appearance. He tucked errant hairs and pulled some strands out, to soften her face. He fixed her hood, so it lay flat. She put his collar up. She liked the way he looked with his collar up, like a man who could rescue her from anything, how he had looked to her in the beginning. Back then, about to finish university and facing a giant blankness, she wanted an ordered path.

Ian turned and opened the door. She was still angry, but she put the anger aside, like a question no one could answer and that she would have to come back to, to struggle with, on her own. They always smoothed things over in rituals. Sara stepped outside after him. She wanted to stop him from walking forward, so she could press her face into his back. She hated and loved his back.

"We forgot to pull the blind in the living room," Sara said, shivering.

"It'll be fine," Ian said. She stood behind him as he locked the door.

"I forgot to give Brittany her goodbye treat."

Ian turned to look at her, as if to check if she was serious. Did he ever look at his female colleagues this way?

"She'll be fine."

Ian and Sara walked across the snow in their courtyard. They were the first to walk on it. Most of their neighbours used the underground corridors to go outside, but Sara and Ian liked to use their front door.

Sara peered up at Ian. A month or so ago, he pulled a tendon in his foot while they were walking Brittany, the day Sara had begged him to come to Riverdale Park with her. They toured the expanse of it, the sun hitting their faces all day, warming them. But then on Monday, Sara had to sit in the doctor's office with him because she was his wife, even though doctors and their offices made her want to vomit.

They went down a street of tall brick houses. The people who lived in the houses, Sara thought, wanted the passersby to see how they lived because they left their curtains opened and their lights on. She peeked in and saw sleek dining room tables, bookshelves, and plush sofas, but the family was always in another room. The family itself did not want to be seen; only the room could be seen. For some reason, peering into one of the houses, Sara had a flash of Joanne. She saw her standing in her living room, clutching her son to her belly. Had Sara ever seen such a thing? She knew she had not.

Joanne had lived 200 or so kilometres away, and when she began to die, Sara found reasons not to see her. Joanne's husband Derrick sent regular email updates. He described visits to doctors and specialists, quoted their exact words, described tests. Sara stopped opening and reading the emails, and Joanne drifted away. Sara went blind, and Joanne's death happened somewhere else, and then she was not there anymore. Her friend was gone. They had met in university, and they were best friends. They went for walks at night in the midnight cold that froze their cheeks, pricked their eyes. They were together so much—took the bus together, ate together, shopped together—that people thought they were lovers. But all they ever did was hug hello and goodbye. There hadn't been any other desire except for the protection of a constant friend. Once, Sara got sick from drinking too many Screwdrivers, and Joanne sat on the edge of her bed and held a cloth to Sara's forehead. She lay beside Sara in bed, her arm over her ribs. Sara slept through the night without vomiting, and when she woke up, her stomach was steady.

After university, Joanne met Derrick and Sara met Ian. Sara lived in Toronto, and Joanne lived in Belleville. Joanne wrote in a birthday card (no one else sent Sara birthday cards) that she could see fields and horses from her kitchen window. Sara and Ian visited once for dinner—a year before Joanne's illness. Joanne and Sara hardly talked. As the four of them sat out in the backyard, and Joanne and Derrick's little boy Jeremy played in his plastic pool, there was an awkwardness between the friends that hadn't existed before, a loss for words. Before dinner, when they were alone in the kitchen, Joanne asked Sara how she was, and Sara said she had a headache from the sun, and Joanne went to the bathroom and brought back ibuprofen, ran Sara a glass of water, and gave it to her. In the light of the kitchen, Sara noticed that Joanne's long, smooth hair had become, in the two years they had not seen each other, almost completely grey. They stood at the sink together, looking out at summer fields, the summer sky. As they stood there, away from Ian and Derrick, the awkwardness lifted. Without saying anything, they turned to each other at the same time and smiled. Then they laughed, a full, throaty, bubble of laughter each, and started moving about the kitchen, Joanne opening the fridge, Sara searching drawers for napkins. After dinner, Joanne showed them around the house. She seemed tired, as if she were carrying a weight on her back. Every room was spectacularly clean, even Jeremy's. He had a toybox so stuffed the lid would not close; the cozy-looking, lifeless animals could not be contained. Jeremy opened his closet so that Ian and Sara could see all his other toys and games. After coffee in the living room, Sara and Ian left. Ian beeped the horn for Jeremy, who stood at the window, his hand clutching the curtains, his white-blond head reminding Sara of the head of a child statue, the kind she had seen in cemeteries. Back on the 401, Sara clasped her hands together, worrying about Joanne's grey hair, the invisible yet visible weight on her back, the little boy.

Sara and Ian turned up the street that led to the restaurant. There was snow falling, but it fell thinly, transparently. A tepid, uncertain snowfall. The city was icy—a snowy and icy mess—and Sara had to hold onto Ian's arm so that she would not slip and injure herself. She wanted winter gone, and gone forever.

They were going to the Pantheon—they served a house red that knocked them both out.

The last time she saw Joanne was at lunch. Joanne wore a wide-brimmed red hat and a red scarf around her neck. Her hair was short and thin, and her hands were like paper. Sara didn't understand the ostentatious hat or the elegant, shimmery scarf, and she didn't ask. Sara asked her how she was feeling, and Joanne said she was feeling okay. Something had gone wrong between them, because Sara wouldn't call, wouldn't ask questions she couldn't bear the answer to, wouldn't drive to Belleville and hold her hand for an afternoon. They were friends, and yet they weren't anymore, because Sara couldn't look at death. Joanne's mauve lipstick was too thickly mauve. There was a smell about her, not sour, but soiled, old, which alarmed more than it offended. She had sent the email asking Sara to lunch, and Sara said yes, hoping the day wouldn't come, but it did. Sara ate Caesar salad and Joanne sipped soup. They talked not about themselves but about people they had known at university, their children, and their jobs. At the end of the lunch, when they were standing in the parking lot, the 401 roaring behind them, Joanne kissed Sara goodbye on the cheek, something she had never done before. Sara was too stunned to kiss her back. Joanne's lips were cold and soft. As Joanne pulled out of the parking lot, she waved from the car, her hand looking too heavy to lift. No one would love Sara the way Joanne had. Sara stood alone in the parking lot, feeling like she had no home to go to.

Ian's boots made crunching noises on the ice. Sara's boots didn't make a sound, because she walked on ice differently than Ian did. She trod on it carefully because she knew what ice was like; in one second, she could be on her back. Although Ian was walking beside her, Sara felt like she was still alone in the parking lot on the afternoon Joanne said goodbye to her. How could she feel that way if she had Ian—bereft on asphalt? He married her. He lived with her and took care of her. But with Joanne there had been heat, a pull they both felt toward the other, an understanding and promise that needed no words. Their faces were flushed in each other's presence. Sara saw flickering in Joanne's eyes and felt flickering in her own.

"You know," Sara said, "I never said goodbye properly to Joanne." The words sounded strange, pushed out one at a time.

"You did the best you could," Ian said. "Nobody ever knows how they'll handle a situation until they're in it."

"I failed her." She tilted her face up to the cold. "She was my friend."

"What more could you have done?"

"I could have been at her side. I was supposed to be at her side."

"She had her husband," Ian said.

She peered at Ian. He stared straight ahead in the way she imagined he always had, and the way she never had, never could. One of his childhood stories was how he had pulled a boy who had fallen through ice out of the black water. He had grown up on a bay, and the bay froze in winter, and the ice was a beacon to children. Ian, at twelve years of age, had performed the model rescue, lain on his stomach and held out his hockey stick for the other boy to grasp. His picture was printed on the front page of the local paper.

Sara and Ian arrived at the corner of the street where the restaurant was. It did not serve the best food, but it was always crowded with either couples or couples with children. Sara had brought Joanne here once long ago, and they'd sat at a table in the back, letting time go to hell, talking, whispering, laughing, filling themselves with food and with each other.

Sara stood for a moment, not wanting to go in, wanting something else. The wind on this street was blowing fiercely, freezing her face, so she could not tell if she was weeping or not.

Vera's Room

VERA WOULD BE ARRIVING in three days, but her room had been ready since Sunday. When Andrew left for work in the morning, I climbed the stairs and stood in the doorway of her room to think about whether she needed anything more. Andrew had chosen the pink duvet, the antique white dresser with three drawers, the ceramic elephant with green eyes, the book shelves. I chose the shade of blue on the walls, the white rug in the shape of a rabbit. I wanted Vera to press her bare feet into the rug every morning and know she was home, that there was nowhere else to go.

In mid-July, Andrew and I had driven north of Toronto to Newmarket to visit Vera for the second time. Vera's foster sisters, twins, were having a pool party; Vera didn't want to miss it, and wanted us to be there. The social worker, Carol, called us early in the morning and told us she wouldn't be able to make it—food poisoning.

We sat on the foster family's back deck, eating rippled chips and drinking Pepsi with ice, except Vera, who had a chocolate milk on the go. Andrew held my hand as if I were about to be executed, or he was. For years, since we married, we endured one thing or another, fought for one thing or another.

Vera wore a red bathing suit and yellow flip-flops that were too small for her feet. Her thick, blonde hair touched her shoulders, and it looked as if it were tangled underneath. Her bangs hung in her eyes.

The twins and their friends—flashes of dripping colour—dove for rings in the pool or pushed each other's heads underwater. Their voices were high and exuberant, and their concentration on the water and each other was so fixed, it was as if Andrew and I, Vera's new parents, did not exist. Jim, the twins' father, tossed rings into the pool.

Under the umbrella, Vera rested her hand on the arm of my chair, as if she were keeping the chair from lifting off into space. Then she touched my hair, the flat of her hand gentle, like an insect landing. I turned to her and smiled, but she was biting her bottom lip.

Her foster mother, Helen, tapped Vera on the shoulder. "Boundaries, Vera."

"Watch me swim," Vera said, and she walked stiffly across the deck, down the steps toward the water. She tossed off her flip-flops, then curled her toes over the edge of the pool. She watched the other girls. Vera's psychologist told us she had trouble regulating her emotions, but she only ever seemed calm to me, as if she thought about everything before she actually did it.

Vera sat down and kicked her legs in the water.

"All right," Andrew said.

He went inside the house for a few minutes and came out in his bathing suit. He did a cannonball into the water, causing the girls to shriek and thrash their way to the shallow end. Then he swam over to Vera. She climbed onto his back, and he swam in wide circles with her. Their voices floated to the deck, but I could not decipher their conversation. Lately, Andrew was as new to me as she was.

Later, we all went for lunch at the Dairy Queen. Every table but one was taken, and there was a din containing the low, steady words of adults and the thrown, wobbly chatter of children. Andrew took everyone's order, happily and authoritatively, the way a president of a company would. Vera sat across from me, and the twins and their friends sat on the other side of Helen.

Jim sat down beside me. "I guess you're not used to all these kids." Then he said, "You two would have made the most adorable child."

Vera unzipped her hoodie, then passed it to me, a red, soft, crumpled heap. I laid it across my lap, and the coat rested there like an extremely light child.

Andrew arrived with the first tray of burgers and fries, then went back for two more. Andrew was always the organizer, the leader. But when he returned, he looked too gleeful and anxious, his neck stretched oddly, his smile showing all of his teeth.

Andrew took a seat on the other side of Vera, and as he picked at his fries, which he always ate first when they were still hot, he asked Vera questions. The outside of her arm touched his, and I couldn't tell if it was an accident, or if it was something they both wanted.

"What's your favourite animal?" Andrew said.

"Rabbits," she said, and dragged the tip of a fry through ketchup.

"Yeah? What do you like about rabbits?"

"They're soft," Vera said. "And they're fluffy. And they're cute."

"What about elephants?" Andrew said. "What do you think of elephants?"

Vera looked off, chewing the french fry, then finally swallowing. "I think elephants are fine."

"What's your stand on giraffes?"

Instead of answering, Vera gripped his arm with both of her hands. "I like you," she said.

"I like you, too," Andrew said, and he spoke as if this were obvious information, old news. "But what's your stand on giraffes?"

"Too tall," she said.

"Maybe you're too short. Ever think of that?"

"Then you're too short, too," she said.

"I know I am," he said.

Andrew then ate his hamburger and Vera sipped her chocolate milkshake, picked the pickles off her hamburger, nibbled her fries. Her mother had overdosed on heroin when Vera was two years old. Her father lived on the East Coast but wasn't interested in raising her or knowing her. One of her parents had given her smooth white skin and eyes that were almost a transparent blue.

"Why are you staring at me?" Vera said to me.

"I was just thinking how pretty your hair is."

"Can I have my jacket back?"

Next to me, Jim laughed, a seagull sound, rippling high above all the other sounds.

I lifted the hoodie off my lap and handed it to her over the table.

During the car ride home, my legs were chilly. I was wearing a skirt, because I thought that's what a potential mother should wear. Andrew wore his khakis and a short-sleeved white shirt. Before we left the house that morning, he scolded me for not bringing a bathing suit. "You mean you're not even going to try?"

"Not a water fan," I'd said.

"This isn't really about you, though, is it?" I had gone outside and waited for him in the car.

He pressed the brake and then stopped for a red light—we were the only car at the intersection, a Petro-Can station on one corner, an IGA market on the other—the necessities. "What are you thinking about right now?" Andrew said.

"Nothing much," I said.

"I know that's not true. Tell me what you're thinking."

"You really want to know?"

"I really want to know."

"She's not what I thought we would have."

The light turned green, and Andrew pressed the gas. Our conversation was on a loop—what we wanted, what we couldn't have, what we could have, what we wanted.

"That's obvious," Andrew said. "How could she be?"

"You said you wanted to know."

"I don't see that we have a lot of choices anymore."

"No," I said. "No more choices." After Andrew said he couldn't bear to see me in the hospital again, we found a social worker, took the classes, passed the homestudy, then waited. After the first meeting with the social worker and psychologist, before we met Vera, Andrew and I had to make a profile book to give Vera an idea of who we were. We put in pictures of ourselves hiking at Rattlesnake Point, pictures of us at Andrew's family cottage in Quebec, a place he couldn't wait to bring Vera to, pictures of our wedding. In the pictures, we were different people, with names already picked out.

The first Saturday in August, Carol, the social worker, brought Vera to us along with her few possessions, her clothes, her stuffed animals, her pictures. We had our sleepovers and visits in late July, but it felt like babysitting: in the end, Vera always left.

After the papers were signed and Carol was gone, we sat with Vera on the back patio and ate hot dogs, salt-and-vinegar chips, and chocolate milk, at Vera's request. Then Andrew and Vera went to the park across the street. Her foster parents had thrown her clothes in garbage bags, so I slid them onto hangers or folded them and placed them in her three empty dresser drawers. I brought her tops to my nose, and they did not have the smell I wanted them to have, a fresh summer smell.

That night, we ordered pizza and watched *Anastasia*, a movie Andrew and Vera picked up from the video store. We ate the pizza on the couch in front of the television, which Andrew said was the only proper way to eat pizza, though we'd always eaten it at the dining room table, Andrew using a knife and fork. Andrew and I sat beside each other and Vera sat on the other side of Andrew. She kept her red hoodie zipped up. She picked off the mushrooms, green peppers, and pineapples, and piled them on the side of her plate so that all she ate was dough, cheese, and tomato sauce. After pizza, Andrew tossed a Caesar salad, and Vera said, "I don't eat salad."

"Don't eat salad?" Andrew said.

Vera shook her head. Then she pushed her bangs out of her eyes— wobbly, curious flickers of light.

Andrew forked the lettuce into his mouth. "Mmmm," he moaned as he chewed. When he was finished with his bowl, he picked up Vera's and started eating hers. But Vera didn't fall for it.

After dinner, Andrew fell asleep in the chair, so when the movie was over, I told Vera it was time to brush her teeth and change into her pyjamas. She took in a deep breath and let it out sharply, but I couldn't tell if it was because she was sleepy or because she was offended. I thought of all her other mothers, the ones who had passed her on, the one who died. On one of her overnight stays, Vera showed us the two sparkly birthday cards she kept from her.

Upstairs in her room, I pulled from the top dresser drawer the new pyjama set I'd bought. The pyjamas were light blue flannel with snowflakes on them—nights could be cold in August. Then I took the pink robe from a hook on the back of her door. I paid too much for all of them, on a high.

"Do I have to wear these?" she asked.

"I bought them for you," I said. "I thought you would like them."

"The colour I hate the most is pink. And the colour I hate the second most is blue and white."

Andrew appeared in the doorway. He stretched his arms out, so that his hands pressed against the sides of the door frame. He looked so comfortable, at ease. Vera's face went soft. She hugged his waist. "Can you tuck me in?"

Andrew cupped her head in his hands. "You have to change into your pyjamas first."

Vera flung around and, without looking at me, grabbed the

pyjamas and robe out of my hands. Then she skipped on her tip-toes into the bathroom.

Andrew and I waited for her to change. He sat at the foot of her bed, and I stood at the window. My back had been tense all day. Vera was seven, but she felt like a newborn, that demanding of my concentration.

"She'll settle in," he said.

"Yup."

I pulled the white blind closed. As a child I had a white blind in my bedroom too, and the first thing my mother did before she tucked me in was pull it closed, keeping the night out, away from me. Then she chose a book from my bookshelf.

I stood in front of Vera's bookshelf with my arms crossed, shivering, though I wasn't really cold. I spent a month visiting bookstores in an attempt to fill the shelf. I slid out *Charlotte's Web*.

The bathroom door swung open, and Vera came into the room and jumped onto the bed. "Tuck me in, tuck me in, tuck me in," she said, her voice high, so that it seemed she was on the verge of having some sort of fit. She pulled back the covers and wriggled underneath them, even though she was still wearing her robe.

"How about a story?" I said. "Do you know *Charlotte's Web*?"

"I don't want a story."

"What?" Andrew said. "What kind of kid are you?"

"I only like stories from you."

Andrew told her to close her eyes. When she did, he began to read the first chapter. He got through three pages before, finally, Vera's breathing changed. I leaned over her and brushed her bangs off her forehead. She had a small mouth, a nose that turned up a little, and wide eyes with light eyelashes, like Andrew's. I turned off the lamp, and Andrew closed the door.

After we locked up the house, Andrew and I usually climbed the stairs to bed. But all day, we hadn't had a moment alone together. Andrew brought a bottle of wine from the kitchen and two glasses. I sat on the couch holding a pillow against my ribs and belly. Andrew poured, then we both drank. Where usually I had coherent thoughts, I now had bubbles, dozens of small bubbles I couldn't keep track of.

Then we heard Vera's voice, plaintive yet insistent, the new voice in the house.

"Daddy," she called.

Andrew went upstairs, opened Vera's door, and they spoke a few words back and forth. Then Andrew turned the hall light on, and left her bedroom door open a crack.

He sat back down, heavily but not unhappily.

"Well," Andrew said.

"Well," I said.

"One day down," he said.

"Yes," I said.

"Did you think it was weird when she wouldn't take off her jacket?"

"She doesn't feel safe."

Andrew leaned back on the couch, propped his wine glass on his stomach, and closed his eyes. "She's ours now," he said, but he sounded doubtful, as if someone might have contradicted him. The long journey of classes, social workers, and homestudy—to make Vera ours—but when would it be true?

School would start soon, so we registered Vera in the one a block north of us, and on Saturday, I took Vera to Sheila's Hair Salon, where I had been going for years. Whenever I had my hair cut, I sat in Sheila's chair, watching in the mirror as mothers brought their daughters in and told the hairdressers what to do, how much to take off and where.

The salon was small and crowded. Women's voices created a dense yet flexible music, the pitch rising and falling, warming, then separating into spare lines.

Finally, Sheila was ready; she led Vera to the chair and I followed.

Vera was squinting out from behind her bangs, looking in the mirrors at the other women, her head tilted. One woman's long hair was separated by various angled sheets of foil.

"I was thinking to about here," I said, and I put my hand level to my neck, just below my jaw. "With some soft, long layers."

Then I sat back down and watched. Sheila led her to the sinks, and Vera sat in the black chair and allowed Sheila to pump the chair higher. Sheila helped her lean back and began wetting her hair, then lathering it. I thought that during the past week, with Andrew at work, we would have grown closer. On the second night, I asked Vera if I could brush her hair, and she said, "No thanks." When I asked her if she wanted to go to the park, she said, "I only go with Daddy." She wore her hoodie every day, watched movies she'd already watched. I tried to teach her how to make pancakes, but she dropped an egg on the floor and wanted to stop. At dinner, she asked Andrew to feed her, and he did, as if all seven-year-olds were delivered forkfuls of peas and potatoes and spoonfuls of pudding by their parents. She drank chocolate milk with every meal, even poured it on her cereal. We went through two litres every two days.

After Sheila shampooed and rinsed, she helped Vera sit up, then wrapped her hair in a white towel, so that Vera's face became a surprising oval. Sheila led her back to the chair. Vera sat without moving her body or neck or head or eyes as Sheila pulled her hair into bundles, clipped, trimmed, bundled it again, clipped, trimmed. Vera's hair fell to the floor around her until the tiles appeared to be covered in light, long brush strokes. Vera pressed her lips together tightly, as if she tasted something sour, and squirmed a little in the chair. Sheila worked foam through her hair, used a round brush with the blow dryer. Then she clicked the dryer off. Vera's hair curled in around her temples and jaw; the ends flipped up. Her eyes were wider and more dramatic—she looked how a young girl was supposed to look, like she was proud of something inside of her. She hardly resembled the girl who had arrived at our house days before with her eyes hidden. Sheila unfastened the cape.

I went and stood behind Vera. "Vera," I said. "Look at you."

"Such beautiful hair," Sheila said. "So thick and shiny."

Vera reached around behind her neck and pulled her hood up.

"Why are you putting your hood up? Your hair looks so cute."

"Pretty girl," Sheila said.

"I want to go home," Vera said and her voice caught me—it was a panicked sob. The music of the other women's voices paused and my face and neck grew warm.

"Okay," Sheila said.

At home, Vera climbed the stairs to her room, and I heard her trip. This past week, she tripped up the stairs twice, and banged into the living room wall, missing the doorway. Andrew thought she was uncoordinated, but I thought she wasn't sure where she was in space, and where other things were in space.

From the kitchen, I heard her close her bedroom door. I expected a daughter who slammed doors when she was angry, but Vera slammed them when she was excited, when she was thrilled, when she and Andrew left the house to go down the slide at the park. The slide was Vera's favourite, though the other kids who played on it were smaller than her. Sometimes, I watched them from Vera's bedroom window. When I was seven, proud of my new height, I obsessed over the monkey bars.

I went downstairs and gathered Vera's clothes out of the dryer, brought the basket upstairs, and set it on the living-room floor. I pulled out a pair of jeans—still warm—and folded them at the knees. Pink ice-cream cones were stitched prettily on the back pockets, but I noticed a belt loop was ripped. Then I plucked a yellow cotton top from the basket. The cotton was worn, and when I folded it in my lap, a chocolate milk stain near the neck caught my eye. Once all her jeans, shorts, and tops were folded, I carried the basket up to her room. Through the door came Vera's humming, high, low, high, low.

"Vera?" I said.

The humming stopped.

"Vera," I said, pushing open the door. "I have some clothes for you."

Vera was sitting against her headboard with her knees up. She still had her running shoes on, and her hood was still up.

"Let's put your clothes away," I said.

Vera didn't say anything. She looked out the window. There were the usual sounds of children's voices in the park, a piano played by several hands.

I set the basket in front of the dresser. The two birthday cards from her mother were lying on top. I slid open the middle drawer where her tops and sweaters were folded.

"Vera," I said. "I think your hair looks really nice."

"I didn't want it that short," she said.

"It'll grow back."

Vera put her face in her knees. "I don't like it," she said. "And I don't like you."

"But why don't you like me?"

She looked up, peered at me, lowered her eyelids, and stuck out her jaw.

I rested her pile of tops in the drawer, slid it closed, then opened the bottom drawer.

"Maybe you and Daddy can go to the park later," I said.

Without replying, she leapt up off the bed and rested her arms on the sill as she looked out.

"You can go down the slide."

I fit her two pairs of jeans next to her shorts, pushed the drawer closed—the bottom one stuck a little—then got up and stood beside her at the window.

"I really want to see your hair. It looked so nice at the hairdresser's."

Vera looked at me. The corners of her mouth were pulled down, and she was frowning at me.

"Stop trying to make me do things," Vera said. Her fist hit my arm, sharp and hard.

Then Vera went over to the bed, lay down, and curled up. I held my arm. There was something not right, unsettling, about the sight of a child curled up with her jacket and running shoes still on. It made her seem like a runaway, someone staying only for a little while. The night before, she'd woken in the middle of the night and sat on the stairs. We both got up. Andrew sat beside her and Vera said she wanted to go back to Helen and the twins. Andrew put his arm around her and said that was nonsense, that he would never let her go. I squeezed in on the other side of her, stroked her arm, but she leaned into Andrew.

"Vera?" I said, and she curled up more.

I hesitated, then I left, closing the door behind me.

All afternoon, Vera stayed in her room. I couldn't reach Andrew because he had forgotten to turn on his cell phone. I sat on the couch, reading but not understanding. I lay on my side. After the surgery, the blooming mass cut out and sent to pathology, I lay on the couch day after day watching *Seinfeld* reruns. The episodes offered a familiar, unthreatening world. Women from my office sent orange lilies, and even though they stood on the kitchen table, the flowers seemed to exist in another dimension. Even when I was still in emergency, and Andrew was sitting in a chair eating oatmeal cookies, and I was lying flat on my back, unable to move without deafening pain in my shoulder, Andrew said, "No more of this," and I said, "We'll see." We didn't have sex for months, first because of the bruising, then for some other reason, some brain exhaustion. We went on with our puzzle piece missing, the room empty, neither of us doing anything until there was only one thing we could do: Vera.

When Andrew finally did come home, I helped him put the groceries away, and I told him what happened.

"What'd you go and do that for?" he said.

"Because her hair was awful," I said. "She was totally neglected. Obviously no one thought about what might actually suit her."

"It was really that bad?"

"It just hung there. It was always tangled. I couldn't see her eyes."

"Still," Andrew said.

Vera came down from her bedroom and sat on the stairs leading to the kitchen. The hood was up. She sat with her elbows on her knees, her chin in her hands.

"Is there a draft in here?" Andrew asked. "Should I turn up the heat?"

"No," Vera said.

"Then what's with the hood?"

"Hair," she said.

"I heard it looks pretty good."

Vera shrugged.

Even though it was colder than usual and would drop to twelve degrees overnight, Andrew barbecued chicken. Out on the patio, we sat at the round glass table. Vera looked too small for her chair.

She ate the asparagus by picking up one piece at a time and sucking the butter off. Then she ate the stem and saved the tip for last. Andrew ate his asparagus with his hands too, making a lot of noise as he sucked off the butter. That she was eating on her own was some kind of miraculous progress we hadn't even asked for.

"She's the only one not eating it properly," Vera said, pointing. For the past week, I was she, or you, or her.

"That's because she has no idea how to be a maniac."

Vera laughed, sitting back in her chair and holding her stomach. Vera had different laughs. One was a breathless, whispery scream; the other was a guttural, low chuckle; another was a melodic, up-and-down sigh. This one, though, was thin and fluty, a delighted whine.

"When am I going to get to see this hair?" Andrew said.

She picked up her chicken with two hands and bit into it. Right away, she had barbecue sauce on her cheeks.

"So for the rest of your life, I'll say, my daughter's the one with the red hood?"

Vera stopped chewing. She squinted at him, suspicious of something. Then she put her chicken down and picked up her glass of chocolate milk.

"You're going to sleep in it, too?"

Vera gulped some milk, set the glass down. She picked up her chicken, took a deep breath and let it out, then took a bite. She chewed the chicken on one side of her mouth.

After she swallowed, she said to Andrew, "Did your baby die?"

Andrew looked at me, as if I knew the answer and he didn't.

"I never had a baby," I said.

Vera peered at me, as if she didn't understand what I had said, and then she smiled.

"Did you want one?"

I took a breath in to speak, but no words came out.

"But we have you now," Andrew said.

Vera giggled—she giggled at all kinds of things she didn't understand.

"My tummy mummy wasn't strong enough."

For a moment, I tried to imagine her real mother. Even though she'd given birth to Vera, I couldn't help but think that Vera was a complete stranger to her.

"I thought we should celebrate our first week together. And so I brought you a special treat. But you can't wear a hood when you eat it."

"What treat?" Vera said.

"It's a surprise," Andrew said. "For after dinner."

"Tell me what surprise."

"No can do," Andrew said, and he leaned back in his chair. Vera gobbled up the chicken. Then she ate her corn with her front teeth, moving her mouth along the length of it, then rotating it and starting again. When she was finished, her mouth was shiny with butter.

"Okay," she said.

"The hood," Andrew said.

Vera leaned back in the chair and rested her hands on her stomach. Then, as if it were not a big deal at all and never was, she pushed back the hood. Her hair was a little messy, but she looked like one of the children in the park across the street. The layers were soft and the ends were wispy. Her hair was parted on the side, the bangs angled down her left temple.

"Holy cow," Andrew said.

"I'm ready for my treat," Vera said, stretching her neck, the neck we could finally see.

Andrew and I fell into the habit of sitting on the couch together after Vera went to bed. Tonight, Vera fell asleep on the couch in her pyjamas, her bowl of popcorn almost untouched, her glass of chocolate milk emptied. Andrew carried her upstairs, and she didn't wake up, which surprised me, because Vera seemed like someone who was always awake in one way or another, in ways I never was. I pulled the blind closed in her bedroom and plugged in the blue night light I'd bought for her after her first couple of nights, when she was afraid of the dark. I pulled the blanket back and Andrew laid her in the bed, and we both pulled the blanket up. Then we stood and stared at her. The haircut had altered her. She looked cared for. She looked more like herself.

After dinner, Andrew and Vera had gone to the park to play on the slide because Vera wanted to see if her new friend, Lucas, was there. I cleaned up the dishes, watched from the window for a couple of minutes, then put on my long sweater and went over. I would go to the park whether she wanted me there or not.

Vera and Andrew were the only ones there. It was cold, but still light out. Vera climbed up on the slide and slid down over and over. She had probably played in so many different parks with so many different families, configurations of moms and dads and sisters and brothers, that it was impossible to know how she saw Andrew and me—as permanent or as full of promises. Our families and seminar leaders and social workers warned us how hard adoption was, how it was a life-long struggle, and when we got through one thing, there would be another, and how we would forever mourn the child I didn't give birth to. It would wear us out—the child, the loss.

Now we sat on the couch, as we did every night after our day with Vera. There was something special about this day, though, because it was the seventh day, and there was no going back—to doubts, to what wasn't.

"I want to take her go-karting next week," Andrew said.

"I need to take her clothes shopping, too," I said. "For school."

"You could do that on Sunday."

I didn't say anything, which meant I agreed, that I was too exhausted to speak. In these late-night meetings, we spoke very little. I always felt stunned by the end of the day, but I was beginning to like feeling stunned, that the person I had been, who always knew what she could have and what she couldn't have, was disappearing. Maybe we were all vanishing, and maybe that was love.

A Boy's Hand

I STOOD AT MY BEDROOM window and watched snow cover the grass in our backyard. The snow falling reminded me of when I was young, though my mother always told me I was still young, but I didn't know it. When I was young, my brother Dylan and I put on our snowsuits and played in the backyard until long after dark; we could see our frozen breath, and our hands and feet grew cold, but we didn't care. We built snowmen and dug tunnels, and I took breaks to make snow angels I would then forbid my brother to step on. He was not like other brothers who picked on and tortured their younger sisters; he did not step on my snow angels, and if my hands grew so cold I could not feel them, he would lend me his Toronto Maple Leafs gloves until I was warm again.

Tonight, my mother was out playing cards, and my brother was out with his friends, the ones he jammed or smoked up with. So I wouldn't be alone, I wanted to go to Jonathan's, and I wanted to ask him for a hug. A hug was the most I wanted, the most I would dare to ask for, and when the hug was over, as I knew it could not last forever, I would command my body to hold on to the hug. My body was a kind of delicate instrument that I could play as I wished.

Shannon and I had been friends since kindergarten, and last weekend, I had watched television with her and Jonathan in Jonathan's living room, and when I got up to get another Molson Canadian, he followed me into the kitchen. I stood at the counter opening the beer bottle, and he stood beside me and blew into my ear, a small explosion of heat. I turned and he laughed in my face, his mouth wide open and his small, sharp teeth exposed, as if I had been the one to sneak up beside him and blow into his ear.

I went out to the kitchen and phoned Jonathan, and he answered on the seventh ring.

"Jonathan?" My voice was gravelly.

"Yeah?"

"It's Tanya." I pressed my finger to a spot on the wall where the wallpaper, a pattern of grandfather clocks with cuckoos inside, had peeled away.

"Yeah." I heard something being banged against a counter, a harsh, clanging echo.

"So I wanted to come over."

"I don't see what the point is," he said in his flat, scratchy voice.

"It could be fun," I said, and wondered if he remembered breathing into my ear, sharing his warm breath.

"How?" he said.

"It could just be fun," I said.

The banging started again, and I couldn't tell if a mysterious object or the counter was being destroyed. Then he hung up, and there was only the drone of nothing and nowhere.

Snow caught on my eyelashes, so I had to squint the way I did in direct sunlight. The only warm spot on my body was between my legs. The snow muffled all the usual sounds of dogs and cars and kids. It was like I was the only person left in my neighbourhood, and everyone else had gone somewhere, but I didn't know where. I was wearing the sheepskin mittens my father gave me for Christmas.

When I was near the top of the street, a car went by slowly, and I peered through the snow to see who was in it. In the back seat, there was the long, frightened face of my brother; he blinked, and I said, "Hi," my voice alone in the snow. He nodded. His face was always frightened, but he never told me what he might be afraid of. A couple of years ago, he plucked out all his eyelashes, and my mother said it was just a stage. The car revved on, whipping up a tail of exhaust.

The last time he was really kind was at the end of the summer, and I was on the front lawn on a towel, tanning in my black bikini, the straps untied. The sun had pressed against my skin for an hour, clearing up my splotches, and when I opened my eyes I could hardly see anything but pale, wavy blurs.

He said, "You're getting burned." I had sat up and seen that I was. He had given me this gift, offered for nothing.

I kept my hands over my ears to keep them warm. On this street, Breezy Street, the wind came straight at me, pushing my shoulders and chest back. I walked with my head down, forward into the wind.

I was friends with Jonathan in grade six, when he moved from Scarborough to our softer outer region with its town centre and plazas and schools and quiet streets. He, like me, only mouthed the words to "O Canada" and "The Lord's Prayer." He had dark hair and freckles, and back then, people used to say that we looked alike, especially from behind, because we had the same waves in our dark hair. But Jonathan was slow. We would sit through the same French lesson in Mrs Robert's class, and when we were supposed to begin our work, he doodled muscled, miniature superheroes in his book instead. The men flew over cities or stood inside burning houses with babies they'd saved under their arms. Other times, he drew headless creatures with multiple arms or people in T-shirts and jeans but with bloody holes in their temples. Later, I wrote the new words—*pouvoir, faire, prendre*—out for him and explained what they meant. Most of the slow kids with their droopy eyes looked different than other kids, but Jonathan looked like everyone else, and he ruled every sport, even gymnastics. He climbed the rope like a tropical spider and could do ten backflips in a row on the mats and land on his feet. I'd seen him practice in his backyard; he did flips back and forth along the length of the grass until it was dark, until the only way I could track his body was to keep an eye on his white T-shirt, spinning like a ball. Being friends with Jonathan was like wearing a special, impenetrable coat, and I had looked forward to going to school, passing him notes that no one else could read, notes that said the teacher had a snotty nose or that the girl in the front corner had pimples on her back. He wrote me notes back, asking me if I was coming to his house after school, or if I loved him. Not knowing if it was a joke or not, I always printed, Maybe, Maybe Not. The closest we had ever gotten was holding each other's hands in front of Jack and Chrissy and Janet (reruns), his hand as pale and bony as mine, but solid and heavy and warm, a boy's hand. His parents were never home. Jonathan's mother was a real estate agent, and his father took the train to Toronto to work. We opened the fridge whenever we wanted. We ate sandwiches that dripped peanut butter and honey.

Then Jonathan transferred to the slow school, and I stayed at the smart school—my mother even called my father to make sure I would, that I wouldn't ruin my future by following Jonathan. Now, in grade nine, I might see him at the edge of the field standing in a tight huddle with other boys while they exchanged money and baggies full of pot or hash. Everyone knew that Jonathan was the town druggie. He grew pot in his closet, and his parents didn't know. He bought and sold.

Then Shannon started going out with him. Her mother cleaned Jonathan's house and sometimes Shannon helped, Windexed the glass—nothing that got her hands dirty. After I saw him the other night, I wanted to see him again because he had been my friend, and what I needed was a friend. Shannon said, "I could live without him."

Jonathan lived in a three-storey house. His bedroom window had brown curtains, and his sister Sandra had white ruffled ones, the kind

I always wanted for my room, to show that I was a girl.

On Jonathan's front lawn stood three plastic pink flamingos. Snow buried their feet and ankles and piled on their backs and their tiny heads, their fragile knees looking broken. His parents kept them up all year.

I walked up the driveway to his house and banged on the screen door with the side of my fist.

After a minute, the winter door opened, making a small sucking sound. Jonathan stood behind the screen door with his head tilted back, as if I were shining a light into his face. He wore his green satin football shirt with the white number eleven on it, with a white turtleneck underneath. He didn't say hello, and he didn't open the screen door. I tried to act like I wasn't freezing, but my cheeks stung. His face had changed. He used to smile when he saw me, but now there was a hard flatness in his face and he looked at me as if I was someone who didn't matter, a person of no consequence in the hallway at school, someone who wanted to exist but who didn't exist and never would.

"What do you want?" he said.

"I came to see you."

"Why?"

"Because." I shrugged, as if I were casual and friendly, but that was the opposite of what I felt; all I really wanted was his arms, the smoky smell of his clothes.

I opened the screen door, taking control, showing that my mission was casual, that I was his friend, and that he could be mine, like before.

"Why the hell are you acting so weird?" I asked, and my voice was sharp in my ears, sharp and fearful like someone commanding a dog not to bite. "Where's Shannon? She said she'd be here." I stamped snow off my boots onto the mat, even though his parents were out with his sister. I set my mittens on a table by the door.

"Who said you could come over?" he said.

Then I saw the rifle leaning against the chesterfield. I had seen it the other night on a wall in the rec room and wondered what animals his father, who hunted up north, had killed.

"You have ghoul eyes," he said. He leaned against the frame of the kitchen doorway and looked through his long dark bangs at me.

"Ghoul eyes?"

"Your mascara's running," he said, and then he actually stepped closer and wiped the skin beneath my eyes with his firm thumbs. Between my legs, I flowed and opened, warm, golden.

When he was finished, he laughed. "Your face," he said. "You look like you're going to cry." He put his knuckle against my cheek, and the warmth of it spread down my face, down my neck, to my breasts.

I shook my head, and he laughed again, a hoarse, punching sound.

"Cat got your tongue?" he said. Those were the words my father said sometimes, during visits.

Then he went into the living room, sat on the couch, and wrapped his hand around the muzzle of the rifle.

"Why do you have your dad's rifle?" I asked.

"Why not?"

He picked the gun up, and I felt my toes curl in. He looked at me, then he pointed it at me. I could tell I was on the other end of a fierce concentration—he was lining me up, getting me in his perfect aim. All I did was stand there, my toes still curled in, my tongue growing dry and stiff, like a chunk of solid wood.

"Ha ha," he said. "Got you." He laughed once, then resumed his fierce concentration. He kept the gun pointed at me and I kept standing there and he kept pointing.

Then he lowered the gun and propped it between his legs. His eyes were open and aghast, as if he had seen something that had frightened him.

"I knew you wouldn't," I said, and my voice, just like in the movies, was a low whisper.

"Wouldn't what?"

"What it looked like you were going to do," I said, in the voice I knew.

I leaned against the door frame. I pushed my hair behind my ears. The carpet in his living room was pink, and the coffee table had a glass top. The other night, Shannon and Jonathan and I ate all the green mints in the bowl on top of the coffee table, grabbing handfuls and shoving them past our teeth, chewing with our mouths open. His bedroom, back in grade six, had pictures of trains and trucks on the wall. We did puzzles of jungle animals, tigers and elephants, together on his bedroom floor. I wanted to see his room tonight, to lie on the bed, to smell the Finesse in his hair, and I hoped there was still some way for me to feel his arms around me.

"It's hot in here," I said.

"I still don't know what you're doing at my house."

"I came to say hi."

"You always go walking in the snow just to say hi?"

"I don't mind snow."

He got up and went down the hall, leaving the gun resting against the chesterfield. If I took the gun, he could take it away; if I left, I would no longer be near him.

He came back in the room with a baggie of pot and rollies. He spread a rollie onto the table, opened the bag, took one pinch of pot and then another, until he filled the rollie. He licked it, closed it, then reached into his front pocket for a lighter and lit it. The beautiful, wretched smell floated across the room to me, and my knees bent, as if someone had pushed them gently from behind.

"Can I have a toke?" I asked.

"What will you do for it?" In the field where kids hung out, boys always got girls to do things for whatever they wanted. It was a joke, but most girls did it.

"I only want a toke," I said.

"Jump up and down twenty times."

I just stood there. There was nothing to say, and my voice was gone.

Jonathan took a toke, held the smoke in his mouth for a few seconds and then a few seconds more, then exhaled and sank back into the couch, like someone who had suddenly lost all strength. "Guess you don't want it bad enough."

I almost took a step toward him, but stayed where I was, leaning against the living room door frame.

He held the joint out for me, a small, smoking present.

I stepped across the living room toward him, tracking wet onto the carpet. My legs moved all by themselves. I reached for the joint, but he moved his hand away quickly. He finished it in three quick puffs.

I stood before him. My mother was far away, tilting her head back in laughter, holding up her glass for more wine. Friday was the night she needed for herself, her friends.

He smiled at me, and he put his hands on my waist and pulled me close, so his face was right at my pelvis.

"Come closer."

"Why?"

"Because I want you to."

"Why do you want me to?"

"Because I think you're sweet," he said. I felt the firm bulge of my stomach, like a pregnant stomach, but I wasn't pregnant; I had never had sex.

"What if I'm not?" I said.

"I can tell you are," he said. I looked down at his head, his dark layers and strict, white part. I had a sudden flash of him playing the trumpet, his cheeks sucked in. I used to turn around from the row of clarinets and try to make him laugh, but I never could.

"I'd like to see your room," I said.

"Why do you want to see my room?"

"I used to like your room."

"You wanna get laid?"

"No," I said, because I didn't think of it like that, rudely and with no kindness.

"Then why do you want to see my room?"

"I used to like your room."

A car went by slowly on the road, and its headlights filled the living room with beigey-grey light, like daylight. For a second, I remembered the outside world, where I didn't have to worry about a gun pointed at me, and where my loneliness hurt but never betrayed me. I had a mother and a brother, a bedroom with elephant wallpaper.

He got up with the gun and went to the window and looked out. I concentrated on the white number eleven. Then he turned around. His high cheek bones made the hollows of his eyes bigger and deeper. I knew he was going to point the gun again, play with my life again. There was only one thing to do with a gun.

"Why do you hate me?" I said.

"You're too disgusting," he said. "I wouldn't touch you with a ten-foot pole."

I stiffened, gulping harshly. I prickled all over.

He stood limply, the way he had always stood, like he was someone who didn't fight, but ducked. He breathed in and out of his mouth, and the sound was familiar, the sound of Jonathan breathing beside me in French, after ten backflips in a row. Noisy, uneven breathing; peanut butter breath. A reminder that he was close, that I had someone else. With the gun lowered and Jonathan breathing, we were both connected by a wire, and our feelings were passing back and forth along the wire.

"I'm thirsty," I said. "Do you have any beer?"

He looked at me.

"For a pig like you?"

Then he raised the gun and pointed it at me, his entire body tensed in concentration.

"I could blow your head off," he said. "And you wouldn't feel a thing."

I had the feeling I could never get away. And for some reason, instead of wanting to run, as I had a second ago, I felt exhausted. The sight of the pointed gun made me want to collapse, to fall to the floor and fall into a deep sleep.

"You better run," he said, the gun still trained on me. "And don't come back, Ghoul!" He did his hoarse, opened-mouth laugh; the laugh sounded like it jumped out of his mouth and that he just had to endure it.

Then I turned and walked toward the front door. My throat was filled with what felt like ground glass, and I swallowed painfully. I opened the door and squeaked the screen door open. There were lights on in other houses, and time fell back into its proper slots, into its lines, and I was Tanya again.

I walked down the driveway, my bare hands in my pockets, flames of sweat dripping down my back. When I turned down another street, the flames cooled and slid off. I turned to look behind me. No one was there. Jonathan would never be there again, following. I was back to who I had been before. I had people around me, but I was alone. That was my disease, that was the thing that kept going on and on, and that I couldn't stop.

I wanted a hug, the kind my brother used to give, making a trap of his arms so I would try to get away, but not hard enough to really get away. My mother would say, "Let her go, Dylan," and he would release me, and the air would grow cold. He walked away and did other things, counted his change or took down posters of trains and put up new ones.

The wind was coming straight off the lake. In winter, lapping waves grew slowly into hunks of ice. And it amazed me how something full of motion could be slowly trapped, trapped into deadness, by slow cold, something no one could even see. In grade six, Jonathan and I used to go skating on the bay on Friday nights. Only the edges of the lake froze, but the bay froze completely, all the black fish beneath moving in a dumbfounded way. I didn't stop to pity them. I was taller than Jonathan then, even when we were both wearing skates. Jonathan's skates were black, and my skates were white, because that's the way it always was. Boys skated one way and girls skated another. Jonathan did fast, show-offy boy stops, and he could skate backwards, swinging his hips professionally like a real hockey player's. The stick he brought dangled loosely in his hand. I did figure eights, over and over, arms out for balance. Figure eights were the only thing I knew how to do, and doing them meant I was a girl, that I could softly flow. Sometimes he held one end of my scarf and I held the other, and he would pull me as far as he could out onto the frozen water, into the darkness. The wind from the lake sculpted happiness on my face. I didn't know the time would end. I didn't know that everything would change because it had to change, and that he would become one of the boys he used to protect me from with his attention, because he was a boy and he liked me no matter what, because he was a boy and he smiled at me as if I had something to give him that he didn't have, like I was someone important, like there was nothing wrong with me at all.

I kept walking. The houses had people inside them, but all the houses looked different, like they were uninhabited, had been left for warmer houses. The snow scared everything and everyone into a hiding place. But I had wanted a hug, and that made the snow nothing. The white fell onto my hair, onto my face. It was covering me up completely, but the snow could never bury me because I was moving. That's what I could do.

When I blinked, the barrel of the gun filled my vision. The gun would live inside of me forever. It had been on the outside, but because it was a gun and it was pointed at me, it had gotten inside. Things that were on the inside never got out. They found a place to live, and when you closed your eyes, they showed themselves. I kept my eyes open. In the streetlight, the snow shone and twinkled, like something innocent. But nothing was innocent. Nothing was what it was supposed to be or what it could be or what I wanted it to be. I breathed in the cold air and held it deep in my lungs. And when I couldn't hold it any longer, I opened my lips and let it all burst out.

Ari

IT WAS AS IF THEY had found themselves on another planet. The sky was brighter, the sun humming. Voices carried, words lost their shape. Peter carried the picnic basket, and Jana the orange blanket. She held it against her chest and squinted out at the Pacific, her hand on the blue-and-white sun hat Peter had bought for her; far out on the water, sailboats glided, dipped. It had been Jana's idea to come to the ocean; she wanted to get away from something by going toward something.

They spread out the blanket—it billowed up—then laid it flat on the sand. They both sat and stared as the water tucked itself into the shore. The beach was full of families, but the shore was so vast it wasn't crowded. Children ran back and forth to the water, their feet kicking up sand behind them. Some dug tunnels or packed towers; others shivered in drooping towels. The sky hung over everyone, a softer yet somehow hurtful, brighter blue, its purity intense. Under the rim of her hat, Jana felt pleasantly removed, disguised, the stranger she was. She unbuckled her sandals, pulled the sunscreen from her knapsack. Peter took off his shirt, balled it up into a pillow, and lay back with his arms behind his head.

"Everything okay?" he asked.

She unbuttoned her blouse to reveal a black bikini top. "Yup," she said, then slipped off her shorts. It felt good to expose her skin to the sun; she felt like something crawling out of a cave.

He turned and smiled up at her, his hand over his eyes. Then he reached over and hooked his finger into the bottom bikini tie. "I like this," he said. "All I have to do is pull."

"I know," she said. She had bought the bikini for that very reason, when she had been feeling hopeful, as she had been these last few weeks. Some greyness was lifting. Jana had told Peter that she wanted to go to the ocean, and that she might after all want to try again to have a child.

She squeezed sunscreen into her hand. She started on her shoulders. It was strange to touch herself in this gentle, slow way. She didn't like doing her face. For some reason, it reminded her of her mother, smoothing moisturizer onto Jana's cheeks when Jana was small. She did her belly.

"I'm ready to have my back done," she said and rested the sunscreen bottle on his stomach. He sat up, squirted the lotion into his hand, and rubbed it into her back, missing nothing. The strength of his hand caused her to move forward slightly.

When he was finished, she lay back with her knees up. Peter propped himself up on his elbows and looked out at the water.

Jana closed her eyes. Children's voices reached her, but unevenly, scattered, riding the wind currents. They sounded dimly like goats bleating.

Peter's sister, Patricia, had a daughter, Ari, and the other night, when they had visited, Ari called Peter Mr Bean, and he watched a movie with her and asked her questions about what was happening, as if he didn't understand. Ari seemed wary of Jana, and Jana was just as wary of her.

"You're sure you're okay?" Peter asked.

"Me? I was just so tired suddenly."

"You can tell me."

"I know," she said, and opened her eyes. It always felt deceitful to speak with her eyes closed.

He peered at her, as if to emphasize his declaration, and she allowed her eyes to close and her head to flop in the opposite direction, as if she couldn't stay awake.

Then he said, "You need to take care of your feet." He leaned forward, put his hand on her left ankle. "I want you to get a pedicure. You know you deserve that?"

"Yup."

For a while he didn't say anything.

"I love the ocean," she said. "I could never not live near it."

"That's what I love about you," Peter said, and she liked the words so much, she did not ask him what he meant.

The waves slapped and hissed against the shore—the wind was picking up. One of her relaxation techniques—on her days off—was to imagine a long, white, riffling wave pouring over her body, receding, pouring over her body, receding again. Usually, she would fall into a deep sleep on her living-room floor. When she woke up, the anxiety increased as the hours passed. She was helpless, Peter was helpless, everyone was helpless, but no one else seemed bothered by this.

On the bus to work every day, she held a book in her hands but gazed out the window. She worked at a private learning clinic. All day, she helped children read, helped them believe that they should never be discouraged, never dislike themselves, and that anything was possible. Then she took the bus back to their apartment, heated up soup or slid a frozen lasagna into the oven. Peter usually got home from the advertising firm forty minutes after she did. Whenever she heard the elevator doors open, she went to the fridge and got him a beer, twisted off the cap, and put it on the coffee table. Her mother phoned on Saturday afternoons to tell her what was new—who was divorced, dead, or dying. She left out births, graduations, and weddings.

Peter turned to her, staring at her carefully, closely; the look was an examination, an investigation. She smiled at him, and he looked back toward the water.

Later, they ate the lunch that Peter had packed the night before. He had fixed them roast beef sandwiches with mustard and mayonnaise and there were peaches and chocolate for dessert. Peter liked to take care of her, and she did her best to take care of him. She had taken the bus downtown yesterday and bought them a blanket from Sears; she wanted to contribute something to the picnic, to show Peter that she really was feeling better, and that she was going to continue to feel better.

"I want to get you out on a boat. I think you'd like it once you were out there," he said.

"I'm sure I would." She cupped her hands over her eyes. The small sailboats dipped forward into the wind, yet resisted it at the same time.

"There's nothing to be afraid of."

She hesitated, then said what she always said. "I know there isn't."

"You're afraid of everything," Peter said.

"I just told you I knew there was nothing to be afraid of."

"We could go today."

She paused, then said, "But I don't know how."

"There's only one way to learn."

"I should take a lesson or something."

"What are you afraid of?" he asked. "Drowning?"

"I'm not afraid of that."

"Then what?"

"I told you I'm not afraid."

"How about next weekend, then?"

"Fine," Jana said.

"We'll need to get you the proper shoes."

"We will."

Then he said, "This guy I worked with once, his whole family lived on a boat. His daughter had never lived in a house, that she could remember anyway. I thought that was really cool."

"It is," she said.

"I think I'd like to have a girl," Peter said. "I could teach her how to do things. How to sail. Hike. I was thinking it would be fun to go on a big camping trip up north. You could teach a kid a lot up there."

"Yup."

"Don't you think so?"

"I said yes."

"All I know is that you need to snap out of it."

"I'm trying."

He didn't say anything, just shook his head.

The other night, after Peter and Ari finished watching the movie, Peter and Jana and Patricia had sat out on her porch, the monkey puzzle trees stretching up, the sound of the cicadas penetrating Jana's skin. Ari had been swinging on the swing set, causing it to jiggle, as if it could come out of the ground, and her mother kept cautioning her. Ari had an intensity about her that Jana was envious of; she stared ahead as she swung, then—without any warning at all, when the swing was high in the air—jumped off, landing steadily on her feet. She looked angry at something. She asked her mother if she could watch another movie, and her mother said no. Ari had gone and stood beside Peter and stroked the hair on his arm. She had hugged him and said she wanted to live with him, and her mother told her to go inside. She had to pry Ari's arms from around his neck. Ari went inside and stood on the other side of the screen and peered out with curiosity and contempt, then she had stuck her tongue out at Jana. Peter had seen this but said nothing, and then Ari had disappeared inside the house. Everyone was careful with her because her father had passed away when she was too young to understand death.

On the drive home from seeing his sister—they were crossing

Burrard Street Bridge with the windows rolled down—Peter said that he felt something was missing between him and Jana; he said he felt lonely. It was always just the two of them, and they never did anything special because there was no reason to. They were going to die alone, he said, and Jana put her face to the wind coming off the water into the car.

A group of children had gathered at the shore in front of them to dig a tunnel.

Everything—the water, the sky, the air—was an even more radiant blue, holding light.

"I just think you're being ridiculous," he said.

"What's ridiculous about me?"

Peter tilted his head, as if he had to think about it. "You give me all this bullshit about how much you love me, but it's all about you."

"I told you I wanted to try again anyway."

"I feel like I'm forcing you."

"You're not forcing me," Jana said. "I want it for my own sake."

"We'll see about that."

After a minute of quiet in the sun, he said, "I just wish I knew what was happening to you."

"I wish I did too."

"I don't know how long I can put up with it."

"No one's asking you to put up with it," Jana said. "I'd be fine on my own."

"The other night, you really embarrassed me."

"I'm sorry I embarrassed you."

"You don't even try. She can sense you don't want to have anything to do with her."

"She doesn't want to have anything to do with me."

"She likes you."

"She stuck her tongue out at me."

"Yeah, she can be a weird kid."

"She's jealous because we're together."

"That's crazy," Peter said. He turned away from her, stared out at the water. Then he took Jana's hand and kissed it. "We'll get through this."

"I know I don't want you to leave me." He had a day's growth of beard. Wherever they went, women were drawn to him; something leapt into their eyes. Jana could see them in Peter's arms with full bellies, smiling bravely, with no knowledge of their imminent obliteration. Peter had fallen for what was inside her in the way he had fallen for her; the child became, the instant he knew of it, his reason for living. Then it had died in darkness. Peter had cried himself to sleep for a week; it was a sadness she had not known he was capable of, a sadness that made her weary, lying next to him. All of it—Peter, the evacuation of the child—caused Jana to feel like a tree that had been picked up by the wind and blown to a desolate place.

Those women also didn't know how Peter said that if something happened to Jana, he would die too. They didn't know how he could sit for days in front of the television, and that he would spend the last of their money on a case of red wine and hardcovers. For months now in the evenings, he sat on a chair on the balcony of their apartment, smoking. If it was raining, he wore his green Taiga with the hood up. He always said that Jana had saved him, and she always told him that he had saved her. What had they saved each other from?

Even though she had not put on perfume this morning, Jana could still faintly smell it on her body. Last night, she and Peter had gone for sushi at a new Japanese restaurant, and they had planned to see a movie, but after eating, had decided not to. Jana said she felt the beginning of a headache, and she thought the noise of the theatre would bring it on, and it would take her days to get rid of it. Peter talked all through dinner, talked while his sushi waited between his chopsticks, dipped it into the soy sauce when he paused. He wanted to spend time with his niece, get to know her. "I want her to know who I am, you know?" he said. Finally they walked home in a light rain. Jana, after seven years of living on the coast, had all the proper gear—a Gore-Tex rain coat, a durable umbrella, and waterproof rain boots—but still the rain permeated. All she wanted to do was get home, strip off her damp clothes, and snuggle under her duvet, alone. She told him that she needed a good, deep sleep, and he had that anxious look that meant he wanted to have sex. Peter kissed her on the forehead, gripped her arms. Then he went out onto the balcony, sliding the glass doors closed behind him. She must have been asleep when he packed the picnic lunch.

Jana watched the water. She didn't say anything more, so he wouldn't, and he didn't. The light was hitting the small waves so hard that it looked like millions of silver fish had come to the surface to have their backs warmed.

"I'll never leave you," Peter said. "That I know for sure." He grabbed her knee and held it.

"I'm getting chilly," Jana said.

He took his balled-up shirt, shook it out, and gave it to Jana.

"You're not cold?"

"You're more important," he said.

"Why am I, though?" She pulled the shirt over her head, breathing in the sweet, rancid scent of his underarms.

He said, "Because that's the kind of man I am. I think of you first."

In the car, she held her sun hat in her lap. She had worn it all day, but the sun and wind had still intoxicated her. She had sand between her toes. It made her feel that she had really been at the beach all day, that she had done something a woman her age was supposed to do. She had soaked up a fine day, and the gritty sand on her feet was evidence.

Peter had sailed since he was a child; for their first date, they had met for a beer on a cold, dry night—rare for Vancouver—and when he told her he sailed, she had decided that he was the man she wanted. Maybe it made him seem stronger and more masculine than she had initially thought he was, someone who might leave her, someone she would have to try to hold onto. He was tall and thin, and he had a way of dipping forward, of choosing his words very carefully, of speaking very gently. The sailing, the adventurousness it implied, frightened her, and being frightened of being left alone was her definition of love.

At the end of the night at his sister's, Jana had been relieved to be finally in the car, the engine running. The goodbyes had gone on too long, and it was Peter who had kept pursuing new lines of conversation, offering to check Patricia's roof, the basement for mold, suggesting outings with Ari. Even Patricia had struck Jana as exhausted, her arms crossed, her orange fleece pullover fading her. She had finally said, "Good night, guys," and moved to the door behind them, opening it out onto the much colder evening.

But then, just before Peter and Jana turned, Ari said, "I have something to show Uncle Peter." She had straightened her spine, pushed back her shoulders, then worked herself into the splits, as she'd been taught in gymnastics. As she did them, she looked down at her front leg, her blonde hair falling into her eyes, and Jana had felt the almost physical pain of Ari's longing for Peter, her need for his attention, to have it wrapped around her. Her small, pale body had trembled—with fear? excitement? strain?—under his watch. When she had finished to applause, crossing her legs and holding her ribs tightly, she had looked up and away, grinning crookedly and dazedly at the ceiling, in some kind of ecstasy. It had made Jana scared for Ari, scared for herself.

Jana squeezed the sun hat in her lap. The windows were rolled down, but she could no longer smell the ocean in the wind.

"I just don't know what I would do without you," Peter said.

"I know," Jana said.

As they drove, Jana made a list of all the things she might buy for the child's room. She imagined red and yellow and blue paint, an oak dresser, pictures of sheep and horses on the wall, blankets, and small, soft clothes.

"I've got some ideas for the room," Peter said.

"I think plants would be nice," she said. She saw a big fern hanging in the window.

"Yeah," he said, and Jana tried to see the fern, the brightness of the green. She would buy it tomorrow.

"Whatever it is," Peter said, "you're going to have to try to get over it."

"I want to get over it," Jana said, and she looked up and ahead. She could hardly keep her eyes open. She was having that sensation, as she had since the miscarriage, that she was outside her own skin, that it was somehow necessary to be outside her skin; and yet this condition filled her with the exquisite, almost excruciating sensation of being tapped all over continuously.

They were on the highway now. The white lines flashed briefly before disappearing beneath the car, almost in rhythm; seen, and then not seen, seen again.

Sis

"THIS IS WHERE YOU LIVE?" Simon asked, and we both looked around my apartment. A frosted window faced Spadina Avenue, and my futon lay on the floor. The kitchen was a small indent with a sink and a miniature fridge with a hotplate on top. The floors were tiled. Simon's face was scrunched up, as though he had just swallowed something rotten.

"Temporary," I said, not wanting to say more. I pulled on my tall leather boots and buttoned up my wool coat. I wanted him to see that I was still his stepsister and not a young woman adrift.

He held the keys to his pickup truck in the air. "Let's blow this joint."

We took the stairs because Simon didn't trust the elevator. He had left Muskoka in the morning dark to pick me up, so he could avoid traffic.

I last saw Simon at his wedding three years ago, when I had flown in from Winnipeg, borrowing money from my mother. After the wedding, Simon had gradually stopped calling me to see how I was, and I had grown tired of sharing my failures. Since moving back to Toronto four months earlier, I had not phoned Simon, but two nights ago, I had felt overwhelmed. I came back from Winnipeg, where I lived for seven years, to feel less alone, but experienced long days without the relief of the smallest tenderness. Simon, his voice heavy late at night, said he was sure it would be all right with Diane if I came for a visit, and because I had no car, he offered to come and get me.

Once we were out of Toronto and traffic, Simon seemed to relax, turned up "Back in Black," and drummed his index finger on the wheel. When we lived in the same house, he had drummed his index fingers on the kitchen counter, his knee, the dashboard, my head.

"I love chopping wood," Simon said over the music. "Raking leaves. Burning them. Remember that? Smelling the leaves burning in the fall?" We had lived east of Toronto in a neighbourhood where the houses were three-storey and had front yards and backyards and chimneys.

Before I could answer, he said, "Wait until you see Diane. Huge."

Soon Simon and I were driving past fields of dead grass, misshapen from heavy snow that had melted.

With his white toque on, he resembled a grown child. When he was younger, he had been diagnosed as hyperactive. He couldn't calm down, ran all over the furniture, lost his breath in excitement. His own mother never came home from bingo one night. Her disappearance led his father to my mother, Simon to me. My father died in a head-on collision in my mother's eighth month of pregnancy. We had lived in the same house for four years, until Simon's father left my mother. That year, Simon threw a desk at a teacher, got kicked out of school, and lived in his friend's basement. Once I visited, sleeping on the floor beside him, using his lumber jacket as a blanket. Then he moved to Toronto to live with his father. The other night on the phone, Simon told me he was studying nights and on weekends to become an electrician, so he could give the new baby a decent life.

"It's so bare up here," I said, peering out the window. Some of the trees at the side of the road were bent from constant wind.

"Yeah," he said. "You can hear the coyotes at night."

"Coyotes?"

"Sounds like they're right on the porch."

"Weird."

"I guess you hear traffic and stuff. Ever see prostitutes in that area?"

"They're not really in that area," I said, though the other day, I had seen a young woman in tight jeans and a short coat standing on the sidewalk outside of my apartment, her face curled up in a sweetness produced only by the worst chemicals.

"Don't you ever do that," he said.

"What?"

"You know. Get tempted into that life."

"How would I?"

"Pimps'll promise you all kinds of things."

"I'm not that stupid."

"Don't have to be stupid," he said. I dimly recalled telling Simon, years ago, that once I had accepted money for sex from a chubby photographer with a sweatshirt frayed at the neck who had walked into the coffee shop where I worked. I didn't ask for money. He left it on the kitchen counter, perhaps pitying me. He had been shocked that I did not own a television.

"I have a job, anyway," I said.

"Right," he said. "The glove store. You like that?"

"It's okay," I said.

"Make yourself a goal. In two years, you'll own the place."

"I'm going to be an accountant."

"Wow."

"When I can. I have to go to school for it."

He reached over and patted my arm. "You're going to be the best damn accountant that ever was."

After that, we didn't talk. I clasped my hands in my lap, and I wondered if calling him had been the right thing. I left Ontario when

I felt I had no one. I worked in coffee shops, slept with customers who fixated on the young girl behind the counter, slicing tomatoes for their sandwiches.

Soon we were on a winding road. Trees hunched over us, and in places a frozen lake opened up and hit me in the chest, but the car felt safe with Simon at the wheel. Although Simon and I were related only through our parents' marriage—long ago ended—I had always referred to him as a brother, and he had always referred to me as a sister. Neither of us had siblings we shared actual DNA with, but it was something else, I thought, a shared history, that might hold us together.

We walked up the porch steps of Simon's small green house and he pushed open the door, causing bells to jingle. Diane stood at the top of the stairs. She was nine years older than Simon, a fact my mother had disapproved of. "She's just using him to have a baby because her time is up. Simon never knows any better." I could bear only brief conversations with my mother.

Diane had long red hair, and dark freckles covered her face. She was wearing jeans with a hole in the knee and what must have been one of Simon's plaid shirts. Although she was eight months pregnant, her legs and arms were skinny. She looked like she had stuffed a cushion up her shirt.

Diane took my coat. "I like your hair long," she said.

"Yeah, you should keep it like that," Simon said.

"Did you dye it or has it always been light?"

"Always been."

"I was out of it at the wedding," she said, and she gulped a laugh.

In the living room, Diane peeled plastic wrap off a plate of cheese and crackers. Baby shower gifts were stacked in a corner of the living room, a soft, pastel mountain.

"You getting all settled in?" she asked.

"It'll take a while," I said.

"You want a margarita?" Simon called from the kitchen.

"Sure," Diane said.

"Give me a fucking break," he said.

"Just make it a light one." She smiled guiltily at me. She took a du Maurier from Simon's pack.

"Jenny?" Simon called.

"Sure," I said.

"Five a day," Diane said, lighting up with Simon's red BIC, always red, since he was fourteen. "This is my fourth," she said, puffing.

Simon came in with the two margaritas. He put one on the table for me, then stood at the living room window, as if he were watching for ominous weather. I remembered him telling me on the night of his wedding that he had not been attracted to Diane in the way he thought he should be, but that it had been time for him to make a decision if he wanted to have a happy life. She had threatened to move back in with her ex-husband.

"It's quiet around here. My apartment is so noisy. Streetcars and everything."

"I don't know how people live there," Diane said. "But you're in the city, I guess. You can walk everywhere you want to go. I used to take the subway when I worked down there." Long ago, Diane had been a math teacher. Now she ran a gardening business in the summer.

"Well, I mean, I'd rather live in a house if I could afford one."

"I'll show you where you can sleep," Simon said. He had never listened to conversations that were not about him.

I picked up my margarita and followed Simon downstairs.

When we reached the basement, Simon said, "She's up to no good today."

He flicked on the light, then took in a deep breath. A green couch, blankets and pillows on the end, was pressed up against the wall, and a black woodstove stood beneath a rectangle of window.

"This thing," he said, going over to the woodstove, "heats up the whole place in winter."

"Going to be cold tonight," I said, wrapping my arms around myself.

"We'd put you upstairs, but, you know, one's the baby's room. All set up. The other one has all Diane's shit in it. You wouldn't believe how much shit she has."

Simon walked over to the corner, picked up two pieces of wood, and carried them back over to the woodstove.

"I can understand how you feel," Simon said. He opened the stove door and set two pieces of wood inside. "What else do you have? I was miserable before I met Diane." He slammed the door shut and locked it. His face turned red and healthy from the heat of the fire.

"I'm not miserable."

"There's nothing wrong with being happy. That's what I had to learn." After living with his father, he joined the army, then quit, then moved from one construction job to another, one town to another, until finally he landed in a bar that offered up Diane. He wiped his knees, then stood. "Well, you'll be nice and toasty down here."

"Yup."

Simon tilted his head back, as if to take me in at a different, more revealing angle. I had called him, not the other way around. I had cooked noodles and tomato sauce on my hot plate. I ate my dinner, then took a bath in the pink, shortened tub. Several bills lay sealed in envelopes on my pillow. After I paid them, I lived on a few dollars a week. My mother used to spread all of her bills out on her bed and figure out necessary payments with a calculator. Being organized and stingy was how she held onto the house after Simon's father left. In those years of Simon's absence, I held my breath in a vacuum of loss.

In the bathtub in my apartment, tears in my wet hands made way for the thought that I still had Simon—not for money but for a vine of hope. Old friends were married and gone, hiding in the suburbs.

"Dad gave us a patch of land for the wedding. Going to make a ton on it. Harvesting the trees. I'll drive you out tomorrow. Take a gander."

"You guys are lucky," I said.

"Yeah."

"That you're so happy with each other."

"Diane's not perfect," he said.

"No one is."

He nodded. Then he turned, and I followed him back up the stairs.

Diane had made pasta Alfredo for dinner. She sat at the head of the table, and Simon and I sat across from each other. Diane sucked at another cranberry juice. Simon was on his fourth margarita and I was on my third.

"Sorry the sauce isn't home-made," Diane said. "He didn't tell me you were coming until this morning, and I don't go shopping until tomorrow. So."

Simon sprinkled Parmesan cheese onto his pasta.

"Told you two days ago," he said.

"You told me this morning."

"I guess you forgot."

"It doesn't matter," I said. "It's good."

Simon twirled the noodles around his fork.

"The stuff you make is way better. I hate this jar crap."

"I'm so hungry," I said, "I could eat anything."

Simon picked up his margarita, took more than a gulp.

Diane put her fork and spoon down. She smoothed her hand over her belly. She was still wearing Simon's shirt, but she'd pulled her hair up into a ponytail.

Simon firmly set his margarita down, and some of it spilled over the edges of the glass. He got up and went into the living room and stood shakily near the baby shower gifts. He reached for a yellow stuffed rabbit, then stopped himself. Then he went out the front door, slamming it behind him. Diane rose and picked up his plate, carried it into the kitchen, scraped his pasta into the garbage, then dropped his plate into the sink with a clank and went down the hall to the bedroom. I waited in the kitchen for everything to pass.

In a moment, the front door opened. Simon kicked his boots off and stomped up the landing stairs. The couch in the living room squeaked with his sudden weight.

"Diane," he said, and I heard, after a moment, the bedroom door open, Diane's footsteps as she marched into the living room. There was the ticking of the clock on the kitchen wall, the sound of a car going by on the road, and low, controlled murmurs. Finally, Diane's voice rose, "Let go please. You're hurting me."

Then Diane sailed back into the kitchen. She put the lid on the jar of Alfredo sauce and returned it to the fridge. Photographs of Simon chopping wood, of the house, of the yard, of Diane when no pregnancy could be seen, crowded the door of the fridge. A small black-and-white one proved the presence of a living thing.

I stood carefully, then went into the living room.

"You have a lot of gifts," I said.

"Too many," he said, not meeting my eyes.

Simon got up, opened a cabinet, and pulled out a movie, *National Lampoon's Vacation*, his favourite since we were kids; he liked to watch it over and over.

In a few moments, Diane came in with three bowls of vanilla ice cream. She set three spoons with napkins on the coffee table.

By the middle of the movie, Aunt Edna was dead, and Simon was cuddling with Diane. He put his ear to her belly, spoke to it, said, "Daddy's here."

At the end of the movie, Simon asked, "So you're alright downstairs?"

"Yup."

"If you're cold," Diane said, "here, take this with you. It's really warm." She gave me a polyester blanket that was supposed to look and feel like bearskin.

Simon turned off two lamps in the living room, then turned on the light in the stairwell and followed me down.

He stood in the doorway, and I dropped the blanket on the couch, crossing my arms in the chill. I wanted to tell him something more about why I had called, but my lips stayed closed.

He moved as if to hug me, then stopped, climbed the stairs.

I found my nightgown at the bottom of my knapsack. I pulled my jeans and sweater off, allowing the inevitable goose bumps to form.

The floor above me creaked with careful footsteps. The last time we spoke, my mother had asked, "Have you met a woman more butt ugly?" She giggled at her own words. "Can you imagine what this child will look like?" She had always told me that if I ever had a child, not to expect her to ooh and aah. She had never wanted children, and she would have nothing to do with mine.

I got the blankets and pillows ready, slid underneath, and pulled the artificial bearskin over top.

Simon leaned against the kitchen counter and delicately sipped his black coffee from a mug in the shape of a plump breast. Diane sang throatily in the shower. I had gotten up in the middle of the night, unable to sleep, and sat at the kitchen table, listening to the noises of the house—creaking, humming, clicking, Simon's cough, Diane's light footsteps to the bathroom, the flush, the footsteps back to the bedroom. I listened for coyotes, their ragged voices, the unloved wild.

"Take you out to see the land," Simon said.

"Now?"

"Get out of the house."

He grabbed his truck keys off the table. "Shall we?" Then he called out to Diane. "Back in a bit."

The singing stopped, but Simon did not wait for an answer.

Outside, the man who lived next door waved from his front porch where he stood smoking. Simon flicked a wave back with his leather gloves.

In the truck, Simon put his sunglasses on. "Poor sucker's wife just left him. It's all trash in the bars. Not that I go anymore. Diane goes sometimes. She's on a dart team."

We pulled out of the driveway, then Simon drove over the speed limit. When I was younger, once in a while Simon would wake me up in the middle of the night. His face close to mine, his eyes wide and bright, always startled me. I would have to remember who he was—friend and not enemy. We'd sneak out, me wearing Simon's old hockey coat over my nightgown. We would drive around in his father's Mustang, sometimes on the 401, sometimes at full speed on the roads north of our town. Once, a pair of headlights faced us, and I realized that for several moments, we'd been driving in the wrong lane. Another time, I crept downstairs to Simon's room, where the air smelled slightly musty—attractive to my young nose. I got underneath the covers and drew on his back. He pushed me away. I had a dim memory of taking off my nightgown and dancing in the way I thought strippers did. He didn't touch me or look at me, he just told me in a gruff, angered voice to get out. The night was never mentioned, as if we both wished the desperate act could be erased.

Simon lit a cigarette with the car lighter. As he smoked, he looked shaky, wound up, disturbed.

"Things okay?" I asked.

He turned to me, then turned away, blew smoke straight out.

"Stuff adds up."

"With Diane?"

"Diane's peachy." Then he said, "Talk to Mom lately?"

"Not really."

"Should," he said. "She doesn't have anyone else."

"True."

"Call her."

"You talk to her?"

"Every Sunday morning. Every week she has something new to cry about."

"What now?"

"John told her to get lost."

"She probably did something."

"Probably," he said.

I had asked him once, when we were kids, if he ever wanted to find his own mother, and Simon had said that he didn't want to find her, that my mother was his mother, that we were a family. We were in his basement room, listening to Def Leppard.

We turned onto a gravel road; trees, yellow leaves still clinging to them, stood on either side. After a few moments, he slowed down and pulled over. I climbed out of my side, and he climbed out of his. Then I followed him down a hill of trees. We stopped in a clearing. When I had first seen Simon at the door of my apartment, he had looked tall and wide and strong, his driving gloves in his hands. He looked like the brother I had been missing. Now, in the clearing, already losing his breath, Simon was shorter, and his eyes were swollen with exhaustion. He spoke quickly, the words bubbling out of him.

He was going to farm the trees. Make money. Build a house. Have a pony farm. Open up a coffee shop where people could also buy magazines. To farm the trees, he needed a piece of machinery that cost as much as the house, and they were talking to a bank.

"Diane's not too into it," he said. "Not much of a risk taker." His cheeks were red, and his breath came out in quick, white puffs.

Up through the trees, the sky hung dimly white. In the moment I looked up, I felt hollow, someone with nothing to give or collect. The trees and sky began to slowly spin.

"How you doing, Sis?" Simon asked. He had always said Sis, like a brother on television. "You look like you're going to fall right over."

"No," I said.

Still, he grabbed my shoulders and pulled me close.

On the drive back to the house, Simon said he wanted me to stay another night. He had missed me all the years I was away, and he wanted to get to know me better, spend more time with me, hanging out. He felt bad for all I had gone through when I was young, with Mom. Once Simon and his father were gone, my mother and I moved beyond bickering to punching and scratching.

"That wasn't your fault," I said.

"When you lived in that boarding house," he said. "I don't even want to think about it." He had met me for coffee a couple of times and given me anything he could—cash, a CD he didn't want. I was seventeen then, but I thought I could not have been more of an adult, living in a room alone, paying with money I earned as a hostess at a restaurant.

"It was my decision." Simon was already living with his father in Toronto, and I no longer wanted to live with my mother. After I lived in the boarding house for a couple of months, I had driven with my friend Shelly to Banff, borrowing so much of her money it was practically theft. We parted at a hostel. Simon's father sent me meagre cheques until I found my way, working behind the counter at a hotel. For the first seven months, I was on anti-anxiety medication. A doctor in a clinic scribbled the prescription after looking at my face only once. In the seventh month, I grinned at myself in the mirror of a hotel room, and the grin, to some distant, interior observer, was the horrific grin of a woman about to be dead. I drove with another friend to Winnipeg, with the intention of going to school to become a nurse, but I recoiled at the thought of touching a sick person's skin.

"I'll think about it," I replied, meaning an extra night. Light snow began to fall, and Simon turned the windshield wipers on. If I left, it would have to be soon.

When we got home, Simon and Diane argued in the kitchen. Diane wanted money to get her hair cut, and Simon told her the hairdresser in town was too expensive and that she could get her sister to cut it for free. If she wanted extra money, maybe she shouldn't be going to the bar three nights a week to see her ex-husband. Diane's voice was high and defensive, but still strained with politeness.

I waited in the living room. Diane had begun to organize the shower gifts into categories: clothes, bath, toys. They were objects belonging to a world to which I could not find the door. Outside, frenzied snow dimmed the air.

In a moment, everything stopped, the radio went on—classical music. Diane had told me during the movie that the baby liked it.

Without a word, without looking at me, Simon put on his coat and boots and a hat with flaps over the ears, and went out the back door to chop wood. Snow dizzied itself around Simon's solid, seemingly impenetrable form.

Diane came into the living room with a mug of tea, the string hanging over the side. She sat in the big, blue chair by the window and adjusted the pillows to better support her back.

"I should have asked," she said. "Do you want tea?"

"I'm okay."

She patted the arm of her chair and told me she had chosen it as her feeding chair, for when the baby came. "I can look out the window. Sleep if I want."

Shame crawled up and down my arms. I had become a woman you passed on the street, a bloodless woman, veiled in confusion. I had become someone who had never loved, because I had protected an awful, weak self that couldn't be born.

Then Diane smiled at me. "If you ever need them, I can get you some maternity clothes." Today, she wore black stretchy pants and a black sweater with a red butterfly on it. "Most of mine are from my sister."

"Thanks," I said.

"I don't even know if you want to have kids," she said. "Your mom always says she never wanted them."

"That's true," I said.

"Simon can't take her anymore."

"I know."

"She's like a little kid if you ask me. And she has no one to blame but herself."

"She is like a kid." A grown woman who sulked and pleaded and blamed, who didn't know it was a decision you made, to stand on your own two feet, even if that was all you could ever do.

I thought of my apartment, the phone resting on the floor beside the bed. I always kept my phone close to me while I slept, as if I expected a call, but from whom I didn't know; someone who would speak words that would cause loneliness to lose its power over me. How could I go home? How could I not?

"You must be wanting to get back to your own place," Diane said, looking out the window.

Outside, Simon had a piece of wood ready to chop. He held the axe high in the air.

Souvenirs

OUR MOTHER LAY ON the couch with two bed pillows propped behind her head. She wore a pink sweater with jeans; the outline of her body was hardly visible in her clothes. She held a crossword book in one hand and a pencil in the other.

My sister, Alexandra, sat in the middle of the living-room floor on the Persian rug, even though Edward's chair was empty. Her dyed black hair was pulled into a ponytail. On her wrist she wore a brown, woven leather bracelet, a gift from Brenda. Alexandra and I had been home for two days, sleeping in the same queen-size bed in the spare room of the condominium. Alexandra had flown in from Vancouver, and I had flown in from Montreal. The bedroom opened up onto the balcony, and at night the sliding glass doors whitened with frost.

Edward paid for our flights. A couple of weeks earlier, he phoned to tell us that our mother believed she was going to die. She had a pain in her side, but the doctors' scans came back negative. When I tried to talk to her on the phone, she said it was too painful to stand or to sit on a chair in the kitchen. Edward told us she wasn't eating.

Tonight, our third night in the condo, Edward went out to dinner with his daughter, Julie, who had been away at Harvard, studying law. When she returned to Canada, they resumed their weekly dinners. On Edward's night out with Julie, we had always ordered in.

"Are you hungry?" I said to our mother.

She looked at her hand, studied the two gold rings. "Perhaps."

"I could make my special salmon," Alexandra said. She got up and switched on the lamp that sat on the end table behind our mother's head.

"You've been talking about that," our mother said. "Brenda's recipe." Then she said, "Laura doesn't like salmon."

"I don't mind," I said.

"Tomorrow we'll have Alexandra's special salmon."

Alexandra stood up. She was healthy and young, but this morning, when we went down for a swim in the empty indoor pool, I moved ahead of her with my front crawl. She had resembled a lobster, all arms, no kicking from behind. Then she went into the sauna. When I arrived there wrapped in my towel, she was gone.

Alexandra went down the hall to the guest bedroom.

Our mother pencilled in a word, frowned at the page, then sighed.

"How do you feel right now?" I said.

"What do you think?" She looked at me sharply, a look I remembered from when I was young.

"It will go away," I said. "I know it will."

"They said it could last forever." She laid her crossword book open and flat on her chest. I hoped she would ask about Stephen, about whether I missed him.

"Chinese?" she said.

"Okay."

"Find out what Alexandra wants."

I knocked on the guest bedroom door but heard only silence. Then the phone receiver clicked back into place, the door opened, and Alexandra regarded me as if she hadn't seen me in years and could not recall who I was.

Her hair hung around her pale, round face. She climbed onto the bed, wrapped her arms around her shins, then buried her face in her knees. She wore the white sweatshirt with "EDWARD" in black capital letters on the back; she must have found it folded in one of the dressers. Alexandra had worn the sweatshirt every day in grade eleven. It was how I recognized her from a distance in the cafeteria, in addition to her stiff slouch.

"What's the matter?"

Alexandra looked up, blinked away the darkness. "What isn't the matter?"

"You don't want to order in?"

"I don't care."

"What then?"

"Being here, with her. You," she said. "It brings back memories."

She grabbed the scrunchie from the dresser and smoothed her hair back into it. When we were younger, our mother always dressed her up, gave her purses and necklaces and gloves. Alexandra's hair had been a white blonde.

"What kind of memories?"

"You don't have to talk to me," she said. "I'll be going home tomorrow." Although the television was inches away from her on the dresser, she picked up the remote and turned it on. A man with a microphone stood before a car crash. She pressed a button and the channel changed.

"Does Mom know?"

"I told Edward."

"Is it about Brenda?"

"It's partly that. It's just so screwed up."

"You mean, she's screwed up?"

"It's not just her. It's her family, too."

"That wasn't right about the birthday cake."

"I know it wasn't right," she said, sharply. "You don't have to tell me what's right and wrong."

She tucked her feet into the blue, knitted slippers our mother no longer wore. Neither of us had remembered how cold it was, even indoors, with Edward scrimping on heat. When we complained, he said everyone in the world now thought you could get through the winter months without a sweater. "Imagine that," Alexandra said. Edward said someone studying psychology should come up with a way for people to keep warm without any heat at all. Our mother said, "Leave Alex be," and he said, "She's up to the task."

"I was just trying to help."

"It would be easier if you didn't."

"Mom wants to order Chinese."

"Mom wants to or you want to?"

"It was her idea."

"Yeah," Alexandra said.

"Whatever your problem is, you're acting really rude."

Alexandra smiled at the television screen as she changed channels. Even as a kid, she overdosed on television, convincing our mother to let her have one in her room. "I'll remember that one," she said.

The delivery man came, and Alexandra paid with the cash our mother had left out. Then she carried the bags of food into the dining room. Our mother slept on the couch, her arm over her face, the crossword book face down on her chest. I opened up all the curtains. The condominium was outside Toronto in Etobicoke, and neither Edward nor my mother would walk in the neighbourhood at night. They moved here to be closer to Edward's door manufacturing company, but didn't leave when he retired. On our first evening in town, Alexandra and I wanted to walk over to the grocery store to buy milk and cereal for the morning, but Edward insisted on driving us.

Alexandra set the table with silverware our grandmother had left to our mother. She wore a long, loose, red cotton dress and had her hair in pigtails. The pigtails made her face rounder and younger.

"Mom," I said. "Dinner's here."

She mumbled, her arm still over her eyes.

"You have to eat, Mom," Alexandra said.

"Not hungry. You girls go ahead."

Alexandra said, "If you're not going to eat, I guess we're not either."

"Fine," she said. "I'll have an egg roll."

"We gots egg rolls," Alexandra said, and she smiled, showing the even teeth that Edward had paid for.

"We gots egg rolls, do we?" our mother said, pushing herself to a sitting position.

"We gots a lots."

Our mother stood. She walked toward the table carefully, as if her hips were rotating blades. By the time she had reached the table, she was out of breath.

"Are you all right?" I asked.

"Pull out this chair for me."

I pulled it out, and she sat down carefully. Then she picked up her knife, examined it, and set it down.

"One egg roll coming up," Alexandra said.

"And why are you all dressed up?" our mother said.

"A gal can't dress up?" Alexandra said.

"I just didn't think you liked to. I thought you were more the casual type."

"Turning over a new leaf," Alexandra said. She pried a lid off one of the boxes and forked one egg roll out and put it on our mother's plate.

"You girls can have all the rest of this. Edward doesn't like Chinese."

"Well, okay, then," Alexandra said.

"Alex, can you grab that other pillow from the couch?"

She went and got it, then helped our mother get the pillow underneath her.

"Time to eat," Alexandra said.

"Laura, grab my pills from the coffee table." I went and got them, and she said, "Some water. Warm."

I ran her a glass of water and brought it to her.

By that time, Alexandra had heaped our plates with rice, chicken, beef and broccoli, pork, and egg rolls.

"Mom," she said, sitting down. "What's something you remember about me from when I was a kid?"

"I told you guys, I don't remember a lot from back then. Those were hard years for me. Living with your father." Our mother began to cut off a piece of egg roll. "What about the time you locked yourself in the bathroom and pulled all the toilet paper off the roll?"

"I already know about that. Try to remember something you've never told me."

"I wish it wasn't all a big blank. How's Brenda?"

"Try. I know there's something in there."

"I remember bringing you home from the hospital. And Laura was waiting for you by the Christmas tree. 'Zanna,' she said."

"Can you remember anything just about me?"

"I remember you crying in your high chair when you had pneumonia," I said. "I thought you were going to die."

"Not sure about that one," our mother said. "We were at Mother's when she had pneumonia."

"You remember that?" Alexandra asked.

"Mother was the one who said we should take you to the hospital."

"You didn't think anything was wrong with me?" Alexandra asked, and put a forkful of rice into her mouth.

"I guess I must have."

She chewed, taking her time, then swallowed. "But it wasn't your idea?"

"What's so great about the past?" our mother said.

"People like to know about their pasts," I said.

"I'll never forget the time the school phoned me to tell me Laura was drunk and that she'd tried to jump out a window." She tilted her head, her face philosophical and quizzical, shrewd. "Do you really think you would have done it? Not a day goes by that I don't wonder about that." Then she rested her fork and knife sideways on her plate next to half an egg roll.

"I wonder what would have happened to me," Alexandra said, "if Grandma hadn't noticed I was really sick."

"You're here today," our mother said. "Isn't that all that matters?"

"How was the egg roll?" Alexandra said.

"I need to lay down. You girls finish this up. Keep the change."

She put her hands on the table, stared straight ahead, and then pushed herself to a standing position.

"Chair," she said, and before I could, Alexandra got up to move it out and away. Then she gripped our mother's arm and helped her walk to the couch. Once they were at the couch, Alexandra said, "The pillow."

I brought the pillow over and placed it where the small of our mother's back would soon be.

"You guys are better than Edward," she said. "Both of you."

As we helped lower our mother down, she let out a "Whew" through pursed lips, then fished between the couch cushions for her crossword book. Alexandra switched on the lamp and snuggled up beside her to do the puzzle with her. They had always done them together on Saturday mornings, using dictionaries, atlases, and encyclopedias. Back then they wouldn't look up from the dining room table until victory was theirs.

When it was dark, it began to snow—a lifting and falling net. Our mother flipped through pictures of a long-ago trip to Namibia, and Alexandra lay on the floor on her stomach. Her pigtails were lopsided. Edward still wasn't home. I always wondered what his

Wednesday nights with Julie were like. Our father had lived with his wife and adopted daughter four blocks away, but we saw him only if we bumped into him at the movie theatre or grocery store or when we visited on Christmas Eve. We brought his daughter presents, but she gave nothing to us. When I was sixteen and Alexandra was fourteen, he bought us hand puppets, Alexandra the frog and me the spider.

"It's snowing," I said.

Alexandra dropped the pictures back into the package—they never bothered with photo albums. "*Touched by an Angel*," she said.

She took one arm and I took the other, and we helped our mother into the den onto the new leather couch, large enough for three football players in uniform.

"Great for kids," she said. But which one of us would ever give our mother a grandchild?

I opened up the baby-blue blanket on the end of the couch and placed it over her. She took my hand and held it, gripped my fingers with hers.

Alexandra picked up the remote, pointed it at the television, and pressed the power button. She went through the channels until pining orchestral music could be heard.

"You wouldn't believe how warm this little blanket is," our mother said. Her mother had knitted the blanket and left it to her. When I turned to go, she said, "There's room here on the end."

"It's okay."

"Alexandra?" she said. "Room on the end."

"I have to make a phone call," she said. The show began. Alexandra left the den.

"Edward will be home soon," I said.

She pursed her lips, stuck her chin out, then peered up at me, as if to assess whether or not I had intended harm.

At the living room window, I watched the snow fall. Stephen had moved out. He said he could not guarantee that he would always be there. I missed watching him shave, watching him eat his cereal and read the paper at the same time, the smell of his neck, like spicy oranges. When I locked up the apartment in Montreal to head to the airport, I looked forward to having other bodies around me.

I sat on the couch in our mother's spot, still warm, the lamp still on. The three of us had always been like this, together but apart. After our father left and before Edward, Saturdays in our house were like church: our mother read the newspaper at the kitchen table; I rearranged my room or drew pictures; and Alexandra sang to her dolls, her voice high and joyful. I had not been aware of any need we might have had for each other.

Alexandra came in and sat with her knees up in Edward's chair, the chair where he drank his red wine and read his *New Scientist*. She wore blue and red tartan pyjamas.

"So you talked to her?"

"Yeah," she said.

"What did she say?"

"She says she doesn't know what she's doing."

"You mean whether she's gay or not?"

"She knows she's gay." There was disgust in her voice.

"Then what does she mean?"

She pulled the easy chair back and put her legs out, her feet enclosed in our mother's slippers again. "I know you're trying to help, but you can't."

"Don't you think you deserve better?"

"We have this connection."

"People always have connections."

"She understands me in a way no one ever has or ever will."

"You made her a birthday cake and she left you there with it."

"You can't understand." She closed her eyes. She took in a deep breath, held it, then let it out.

"You think I've never loved anyone?"

She opened her eyes. "But has anyone loved you back?"

She brought her wrist to her nose and smelled her leather bracelet. "It's not a real relationship unless they love you back. Otherwise, it's just an infatuation."

"Stephen said he did."

"But do you really think he did?"

"I do everything I can to understand you, and you don't do anything to understand me."

"Is that right?"

"You think everything's easy because I'm not gay?"

Alexandra put her hands over her face.

I felt sick to my stomach as I always did when I hurt her. One summer, our mother went to South Africa with Edward for six weeks to meet his family and left us in our father's care. In a rented Winnebago, our father took his wife and daughter and us to Florida. One night, Alexandra told me that people at school thought I smelled, and that I should change my clothes once in a while. I told her two days later, after thinking it through, what our mother told me: when I was born, she found her reason to live. Alexandra had lain still beside me, then said in a whisper that I was lying to get her back for what she had said about me smelling, but we knew what kinds of lies the other was capable of and what would have been simply beyond either of us.

Later, we went back to the den. Our mother was asleep on her back, her mouth open as she breathed. The blanket was tucked up around her neck.

I leaned over her and squeezed her arm. "Time to go to bed."

She startled, gasped, then gazed at me in the dark, her face open and vulnerable, the other side of her, a side only Edward could have known.

I pulled her to a sitting position. Carefully, she rotated, so that her feet were on the floor. Then she pushed herself up. "I'm all right," she said.

Alexandra and I each took an arm and walked her to the bedroom. Our mother went into the bathroom alone and closed the door. She groaned, then was quiet for too long. When she came out, she was wearing a brown satin nightgown, something Edward brought back years ago from a trip alone to New Jersey. The bones in her chest showed.

She sat on the edge of the bed. The side she slept on was higher because a piece of foam had been laid down on it.

"Edward put this in for me," she said. Neither Alexandra nor I asked why he was still not home. The bedroom seemed to belong only to her, with containers of lotions and glass perfume bottles, mirrors and brushes spread across the dresser, objects from the middle of her life, when she had at last found love.

"Pills," our mother said, and Alexandra went and got them.

"You guys always got along when you were younger," our mother said.

Alexandra stood in the doorway with the bottle of pills and a glass of water.

"Did you make sure it's not cold?" I said. "She doesn't like it cold."

"It's fine," our mother said.

I took the pills, opened the bottle, and pressed one into our mother's hand. "Two," she said. I gave her another one, and she clapped her palm up to her mouth, then held her hand out for the water.

"You want some lotion?" Alexandra asked, and her voice wavered. We hadn't looked at each other once since we saw her body.

"On the dresser. Aloe vera. I like the smell of it."

Alexandra went to the dresser and squeezed a mound of lotion into her hand. "Where do you want it?"

"Maybe my shoulders."

"I hate dry legs," I said, and squeezed lotion into my hands. I knelt, smoothing lotion onto one of her legs, then the other. "They get so itchy."

"Then you can't sleep."

"It's dry in here," I said.

"Humidifier's back in the laundry room. Underneath some lawn chairs."

"I'll get it for you," Alexandra said.

"There," I said, as if I were proud of something, but when I'd touched her skin, I failed to absorb her.

Alexandra dragged the humidifier out on its ancient wheels. She plugged it in beside the dresser, then turned it on, loud and chugging.

"And what about you?" our mother asked. "How are you really doing?" She meant Stephen.

"I feel what I feel."

"But that isn't necessarily good."

Alexandra left the room.

I pulled her blanket back and helped her lift her legs up into the bed. There was no way to say what it felt like to be alone—when I was supposed to be shoring up and securing essential belongings, I was still searching for them.

"You'll be okay," she said. "I always knew you would be."

She sounded as if she was having difficulty getting the words out in a straight line, getting them past her teeth and lips; she sounded tipsy. I took her glasses off and rested them on the night table. I had seen her so rarely without them that I felt like I had removed part of her face; the eyes that were left searched the darkness, then rested on me.

"How do you know I'll be okay?"

"I just know you will be."

"But how can anyone really know that?"

"I just look at you. I've never doubted it."

"But what if I wasn't going to be okay?"

She took my hand, held it lightly. She closed her eyes, smiling. The pills had kicked in; on the phone, she'd said that when the pills began to work, she felt that she was floating.

Alexandra was already in bed, reading a book about Egypt, one from Edward's pile. Sometimes it seemed she was his actual daughter.

"You always have to win," Alexandra said.

"Win what?"

"I called Brenda. She's picking me up from the airport." Then she said, beaming, "And she says she has a surprise for me, something I'll never guess, and something she's never done for anyone before."

"How is Mom supposed to see you?"

"The pain will stop when she wants it to stop."

"You've got to be kidding me."

"She probably feels it because of guilt, for not taking proper care of us when we really needed it."

"You think she wants this?"

"Not consciously."

I changed into my sleeveless, black cotton nightgown and got into bed. In my bed in my apartment, without Stephen breathing beside me, I could hear the elevator going up and down late into the night, the ecstatic, drunken revellers.

Alexandra closed her book and placed it on the tall dresser beside her, the one she had as a teenager. She turned out the green desk lamp that used to be in my room. I would fall asleep beneath its gold heat, writing letters to my father. I wrote them on blank, blue-coloured paper our mother brought home from the office. Edward, a door salesman then, had walked into an office one day and was greeted by our mother, the receptionist. She told the story over and over again.

Alexandra turned on her side, facing away from me.

My childhood dresser was at the end of the bed. The seashell jewellery box was still on it, full of bracelets and earrings, gifts from Edward's solo trips that I could not bear to investigate, the plastic decorations of my adolescent arms and ears. Sometimes, when our mother went with him on trips, she admitted to buying our souvenirs last-minute at the airport or forgetting all about them as she and Edward toured markets and visited villages and strange cities. Once, she gave me a small white paper bag that said "New York" in red letters. She had eaten popcorn from it while waiting for a connecting flight to Toronto.

When Alexandra and I left for university, our mother and Edward sold the house. She cleaned out our rooms, sold our clothes, CDs, books, shoes, hats, and scarves at a giant garage sale, the first she had ever had. All our lives, she said how one day she would put everything, all of the objects we seemed hell-bent on accumulating, out onto the driveway to sell. We were messy, and she couldn't wait for us to leave. She kept the dressers and my lamp for the guest bedroom at the new condo.

How did the jewellery box survive the jettison? Perhaps she liked the look of it; tiny shells glued to red velveteen. She had brought it back from a trip to Florida, her first trip with Edward, before we had met him. Perhaps she had always wanted the jewellery box for herself.

The gold curtains hanging in the guest room were brought from our mother's old bedroom. After school, Alexandra always napped behind them as if being enfolded in the curtains was the closest she could come to being enfolded by our mother.

I did remember going to school drunk, getting caught in Home Economics when I cut up my orange-and-white-checkered pillow with scissors. Mr Hughes made me stay in his empty grade seven classroom while he went to get the principal. I leaned out the window, gazed at the wet pavement below, and wondered if it might actually feel good to have my whole body smack against something so hard, if it would snap me into better feelings. Then the principal's large, heavy hand landed gently on my back. At the time, our mother was in Turkey with Edward. She paid a friend from her euchre club to live with us for three weeks. Our father wouldn't take us.

The bedroom was very warm, and the heat worked on my body like an intoxicant. Edward must have turned up the heat before leaving.

When she was little, I used to invite Alexandra to sleep in my bed. She could bring every stuffed animal she owned, animals that had travelled with her since the beginning of her life—the purple turtle, striped snake, pink walrus, and the golden retriever. Maybe our mother, after choosing me as her reason to live, didn't need a second, yet she had enjoyed the undeserved, unsought privilege of being the first reason, for both of us.

The room was very quiet. I was trying to stay awake so that I could hear Edward's key in the door. But soon all I heard was Alexandra softly sniffling, swallowing. I didn't know what Alexandra's memories were. Perhaps I was a thief in them, stealing again and again the thing I never once possessed.

Correct Caller

MICHELLE ARRIVED AT THE Petro-Canada station before him. She opened the booth with her key, then made the coffee. As it percolated, she leaned into the small mirror at the back of the booth and wiped the sweat from her forehead. It was Saturday morning, and her mother had been asleep when she left the house.

A little later, Russell pulled into the parking lot of the plaza across from the gas station. On sunny days, he parked his blue Golf under a row of trees so that the car would not be stifling at the end of the day when he faced the long drive home.

He pulled open the door. "Hello," he said to Michelle through tight, sneering lips, as if she had done something wrong. His shirt was rumpled, and he appeared not to have showered. His brown hair was flat. Perhaps he and Pamela had been fighting all night. The pores of his skin were visible, like the pores on a leaf were visible, and he looked like a walking dead man. Michelle saw Pamela once behind the glass of her car window when she dropped Russell off because his car was in the garage. She spiked her short blonde hair with gel and had chubby cheeks.

Russell searched through the papers on the counter beside the cash register, then sighed heavily. "Jeez." The smell of his aftershave, spicy and cold, travelled through the air of the small booth. His skin glistened. It was unusual for him not to dig his fingers quickly into her waist to surprise and tickle her, or to lift up her ponytail and give her a warm, damp kiss on the back of her neck. Russell sometimes laughed after the kiss, in such a way that she thought she was the one who had done something daring.

"What's wrong?" she asked.

"The wife," he said.

"What about her?"

"She wants to have another kid." He poured a cup of coffee into his Rolling Stones mug. Michelle didn't really want to have sex with Russell, but she liked the idea that he liked her; she was the pivot that he rotated around, needed to be connected to, the one that made him feel good about himself.

"All women want to do is have babies," he said. "Why is that, Michelle?" He sucked coffee from the mug.

"I don't want to have a baby." Her two friends, Shannon and Tanya, didn't want them either.

He swallowed luxuriously. "Liar."

"I don't."

"Then there must be something wrong with you." He rubbed her shoulder. "I mean, you're a very beautiful girl. I think you're going to have a baby like everyone else."

"I doubt it."

"Are you a man-hater?"

"No," she said.

"A lesbian?"

"No," she said quickly.

"Sounds like it."

"I just don't know if I want them," she said.

"You know that you're full of it."

He rubbed her back. The sensation of his hand there, rubbing it firmly, made Michelle want to give something up, some longing, some idea she had about how her life should be: a straight line heading toward the future. Mrs Marshall, her grade ten science teacher, told her she could be whatever she wanted. She wanted to be either a pediatrician or a psychologist.

He dropped his hand to his side. "I wish I'd married you," he said. He had said this before, but he would always laugh after, so she never took it seriously.

"Why?"

"Because you're so good."

"How am I good?"

"That's a good girl." Russell's voice grew soft and quiet, and he gave the impression that he was just about to stumble on each of his words, as if speaking were difficult for him.

A station wagon pulled up; a woman in a pink bikini top and shorts got out as a little boy and girl waited in the back seat. Michelle's town was full of women coming in for gas with their kids on weekdays and Saturdays, as if they were constantly on a vacation. Her mother always had to work—she was a receptionist at a dentist's office—and she called women who didn't a bunch of lame-brains.

"Fucking wagons," Russell said, and the door buzzed as he left.

That night, Michelle slid beneath her sheets, and she lay stiffly in bed and listened as her mother, her face brilliant with the Nivea she wore at night, locked both the front door and the back. In the evenings, Michelle and her mother ate dinner together at the kitchen table, then her mother changed into her pink, terrycloth sleeveless lounge dress and sat in the living room with the newspaper while Michelle crouched in a lawn chair in the dimming light of the backyard, reading one of her novels: right now she was reading *Wuthering Heights*. After reading the newspaper and drinking her three glasses of French Cross, her mother lay on the couch and snoozed. When it got too dark to read, Michelle sat at the kitchen table, sipping tea and listening to Q107; she waited for a contest to begin, so that she could, if she dialled rapidly enough, win tickets to see a concert. If she was in the kitchen when her mother came in to get herself a glass of warm water before bed, her mother might say, "Don't look so glum," when Michelle was not glum, and it was really her mother who was never happy, even though the wine made her giddy for an hour or so, before she started talking about Michelle's father, how he had taken the walnut cabinet, the crystal decanters, the silver. She would catch Michelle's attention if she came in from outside to go to the bathroom, but Michelle couldn't remember any of these precious items, because her father had left when she was four. Michelle couldn't have cared less about any of it. In the photograph she had of her father, he stood at the helm of a sailboat. He was a rotund, white-haired stranger. She knew he owned a car dealership.

The wind caused the panes of glass in her window to bang and thump, and the sound of the banging filled her with the sense that she was going to die no matter what, that it was something she couldn't help. The feeling was happening more and more. Her eyes remained dry, but her back became hot and sweaty with fear, that deep fear, like an uncontrollable fire within her, urging her to do something, but she didn't know what. She curled up into a ball. She breathed deeply and noisily and prayed to God to let her live until she was old. Please God. Please. She lay in bed and felt the sweatiness turn cool, and she stretched out. Russell started to flash in her mind in a way he hadn't before: heavy, wide shoulders; his grin. And even though her muscles, the entire exhausted length of her, had begun to feel as heavy as mud, her hand went between her legs, and she crept a finger into her underpants. It was his hand, his. And in her mind, Russell became a comforting, aggressive force that wouldn't let her go.

The next day, Russell came in late because he had got stuck in traffic on the 401. His face was blotchy and red, and the thinning hair on top of his head was damp. Patches of perspiration showed through his white shirt. He had already told her his car didn't have air-conditioning; he had told her all the problems with his car: the transmission, the fuel pump, the worn-out brake pads. He sliced open the plastic wrapping on a Danish, then ate it in big mouthfuls. He swished the food around in his mouth with coffee as he chewed, and she cringed because it forced her to think of his other bodily functions: Russell washing himself, brushing his teeth, rolling his socks on. His wife must have had to turn a blind eye to all of it because she could not possibly enjoy that side of a man.

"How was your night?" Michelle asked.

"Decent. No catastrophes on the radar. You?"

"Fine," she said. "Boring."

"You're sixteen and you had a boring night? Something must be wrong with you." He wiped the crumbs from his mouth. "If I were your boyfriend, I'd show you a night on the town."

"I don't really have a boyfriend."

He poured himself more coffee. He leaned in close to her; he smelled like sweat and garlic.

"I'll tell you something, Michelle, a basic truth of life. What men want is a whore in the bedroom and an angel everywhere else."

Michelle swallowed. She tried to think of something to say. He looked at her intensely; his eyes were like tarnished dimes. "Nice dress," he said. "You're all dressed up today."

"Thank you," she said. "I felt like it." She wore a white cotton sailor dress. She had pinned two sun-streaked curtains of hair back with red barrettes. She wore her mother's leather sandals. A thin, gold bracelet sat loosely on her wrist. This morning, for whatever reason, she had wanted to look grown up.

"You look real classy. You going somewhere tonight?"

"I wish," Michelle said.

He read figures off a bill he had picked up off the counter.

"Oh yeah," he said. "No one to take you out?"

"No."

He stared at the bill; he appeared dizzy and surprised.

"So you want to go out for dinner."

She swallowed again. "Yes."

He put the paper on the desk, turned his back to her, shrugged generously.

"I'll take you out. Tonight. The wife has a class. Swimming for toddlers or some shit." Russell turned around, and Michelle could see that his lips were curled in, his chest stuck out.

"Where?" she asked, to keep the conversation going.

"Pizza Hut. You like Pizza Hut?"

"I do," she said.

"We'll go right after work."

The rest of the day, Russell seemed angry with her, as if she had forced him to ask her out and to betray his wife, even though it was only dinner.

"Is something wrong?" she asked.

"Nope," he said, his shoulders rounded over his work. The rest of the day, she felt herself trying to walk more carefully.

The Golf was too hot even though it had been in the shade. She felt a slight physical danger once she was in the car with him, an occasional shudder that she hoped was not visible to him.

She had called her mother and told her she would be home later because she was going out with her friends, Shannon and Tanya, and her mother said, "Don't have too good a time." She liked to correct and warn Michelle. But Michelle hung up.

In the car, a blue box of Kleenex sat between them, as well as an open package of Jujubes.

"She loves those," he said.

Michelle had been seeing everything through a dark screen. His hands on her shoulders hadn't meant he would promise anything.

Pizza Hut was full of families. Little kids chomped on slices or wriggled in their seats. Others shouted and ran in the aisles. She followed Russell to a booth in the corner. The window offered a view of the intersection: cars turned right to the Town Centre, left to the Superstore. Her mother could make the turns in her sleep. On Sundays, Michelle and her mother grocery shopped at the Superstore, and her mother, with the grocery cart in front of her, transformed. She lingered in the aisles, picking up packages and reading the lists of ingredients. She spoiled herself with shortbread cookies and encouraged Michelle to treat herself to something. Michelle usually bought a giant Oh Henry! bar or the biggest tub of Neapolitan ice cream. Her mother was different at the Town Centre because she refused, on principle, to buy herself new clothes. She preferred to make the skirts, blouses, and pantsuits she had last. But she would try on dresses and say, "Imagine where I might wear this. Imagine the woman who would buy this." Michelle worked at the gas station so she could buy her own clothes.

Russell hunched over the table and tapped his fingers on it. He had long black eyelashes, like a dog's.

Michelle picked up the short glass vase and smelled the single pink carnation.

"Carnations don't have a scent," he said.

"They smell like grass."

"They don't have a scent."

"This one smells like grass." Michelle held the vase out to him. He ignored it.

"It may smell like grass to you, but they don't have a scent."

She set the vase neatly back in the centre of the table.

"I'm hungry," she said. She looked out at the intersection; four cars made smooth lefts, then the light changed to a solid green.

"My stomach's upset," he said.

"Why?"

"Stress."

"What are you stressed out about?"

"Things don't always turn out as you plan."

"Like what?"

"I don't want to burden you."

"You wouldn't."

"Pamela," he said.

"What about her?"

"She thinks—she thinks she's had enough of me."

"Why?"

"Can't you tell?"

"Why?"

"Moolah," he said, and he rubbed his fingers together. "Not enough moolah."

The skinny, wheaty waitress with light hair was coming toward them, but Michelle had time to say quickly, "That's one thing I don't care about."

The waitress had a high voice and a tinkling laugh.

Russell ordered spaghetti and meatballs and she ordered a small pizza with pepperoni and mushrooms and a large Pepsi.

"Gross," he said.

"What?"

"Mushrooms on a pizza. Have you been talking to my wife?"

"No."

Russell sighed and looked off to the side at two little boys hiding under the table of an empty booth.

"I don't know about you," he said.

"Maybe I don't know about you either," she said.

Russell looked at her, startled, then told her to settle down.

"Do you like working at the gas station?" he said.

"It's okay," she said.

"Anyone ever tell you, you look like a bird? Maybe you're a bird.

Chirp, chirp. Actually, you do look like a bird."

"I don't look like a bird."

"Yeah, you do." He laughed in a weak, huffy way, an engine sputtering out.

"Do you like working at the gas station?" she asked.

He laughed. "Yes, it's always been a dream of mine."

He took a long sip of ice water, smacked his lips. "My father thought I was stupid. I applied to be in the army. They rejected me and told me it was because I'm stupid."

"You're not stupid. Not that I can see."

"He's dead," he said. "The old guy is dead." He smirked.

Michelle peered out at the intersection. A line of cars waited for a red light to flash green. Fourth in the line-up was her mother's blue Grand Prix. At the wheel, her mother looked small, almost like a child. If Michelle were in the passenger seat beside her, she would be trying not to listen as her mother listed her resentments and worries: *left us without anything, thinks of himself, lives the high life, I could lose the house, lose the car, lose my dignity.*

The waitress brought their food. Russell ate his spaghetti and she ate her greasy pizza. They didn't talk. When she was finished the pizza, she drank her Pepsi.

"You like Pepsi?"

"Yup," she said.

"You're a real smart broad," he said.

He folded his hands before him and studied them.

When she peered out at the intersection again, cars were heading straight through a solid green light. The blue of the sky had deepened. Her mother must have already gone to the Superstore and then home again, without Michelle noticing. Her mother must have wanted a treat.

"Past your bedtime?" Russell asked.

"I don't have a bedtime."

"Don't have a bedtime?" He sat back, stuck his chest out.

She shook her head. The pizza was leaden in her stomach, and the Pepsi sloshed around.

"I'll drive you home," he said, covering his plate with a napkin, as if to bury it. She had never seen anyone do that.

After Russell paid the bill, they went to the car. The night was warm, but Michelle could still detect a delicate cool, wisps of it on her skin.

In the car, Russell gave Michelle the package of Jujubes. "She won't notice if you only take one."

Michelle selected a black one and sucked on it to make it soft.

Only a few cars were speeding along the highway that cut through their town. The Canadian Tire was still open. Michelle had applied to be a cashier, but she had never heard back and then Russell had hired her right on the phone; he said he knew exactly who she was from the sound of her voice.

Michelle fell into a happy daze—she couldn't remember the last time she had felt so careless. The sky grew darker, but nothing would happen to her, not in this car with Russell. So much of what she saw—the two Shells on opposite corners, Linda's Lovelace, Squareboy Pizza beside Bay Ridges Ice-cream Parlour, the GO-train tracks—was familiar and soothing.

Russell turned onto West Shore, and at the end of West Shore was the lake. Right now, the water was no more than a promise in the dark, and she felt a tremor, an excitement at how easy things could be.

"I love the lake," she said. Then she added, "I never get to see it at night."

"Why not?"

"The roads aren't lit up."

"You afraid of the dark?"

"You just can't see along the road."

"You want me to take you there?"

"I'd like to see it at night."

He cleared his throat. "Am I your new boyfriend?"

"You have a wife."

"That doesn't stop some girls."

"Oh."

He rested his thick hand on her knee, and the warmth of it went right through the material of her dress. She looked out the window to try and think about what she was doing, where she was.

"Just show me the way," he said.

"To the end of this road, then turn."

Soon, the wheels of the car kicked up gravel, a sound that filled her with fear: her stomach leaped and dropped. She caught glimpses of the lake through the trees. Russell parked in a gravel indent bordered with tangled shrubs. She could hear the water, a slushing hiss, but she could not actually see it. She wanted not just to hear and smell it, but to witness it, to drink it up with her eyes and hold the picture there: the lake might be different in the years to come. She thought she saw black waves through the shrubs.

A group of teenage boys wandered behind the car. Kids were always around near the lake, getting into trouble. Bottles clinked.

"I hope you score, dude."

Russell let out a weak laugh. "Tough guys," he said, audible only to her. She did not turn, but kept her head very still in case she knew them. A glimpse of her familiar face would encourage them to humiliate her. She knew who they were, boys who went to the school for slow kids, who hated girls who were smart.

He put his hands on the wheel, a deliberate manoeuvre, she could tell.

"I can't really see it," she said.

"See what?"

She let out a breath. "The lake."

"You want to write a poem about it? The waves lapped methodically," he said. "How's that?"

"It's okay." She had told him she wrote poems.

He bent over and took a bottle of rye out from under the seat, three-quarters full. He sipped straight from the bottle and passed it to her, and she took sips too, sips that scoured her throat, numbed her lips, soaked her brain, as straight booze always did.

Over the day, dark bristles on Russell's face had grown in, so that he was more mannish and alien to her than before, and he brimmed with aggression, talking louder, spreading his legs, and leaning back. He seemed to have escaped something. He clicked on the ignition, so that her station was on. A contest played out. A giddy, stoned-sounding girl named Nicole had won tickets to the Van Halen concert.

The caller giggled in a dozy way into the phone. "This is the best thing that's ever happened to me."

The announcer said, "Do you live under a rock?"

Although Michelle always phoned in for the contests they had at night, she had never been the correct caller.

The rye continued to burn in her throat and chest. Her chest had filled with frenzied worms. Any resistance she may have been sustaining was weakening, and she began to want things for the sake of wanting them. She got ready to shut a door in herself, a door that, once closed, allowed her to feel things but not to know them. She had done it once before, at a party, in the laundry room. The boy was in her class, but she never spoke to him again because she didn't like his bushy hair, and he had a permanent yellow crust in his eyelashes.

She picked up Russell's heavy, hairy hand.

He squeezed her fingers.

"I know what you want," he said.

"What?"

"It makes your pussy squirm," he said.

She leaned into him and he leaned into her. Their tongues were entangled, his slimy, cool, and pointy. He was pushy, but she went along with it. He laughed derisively when, after she lifted up her dress, he saw her lace bra and underwear, her one matching pair. Then he worked his fingers inside them. She hardly had a chance to touch him before they were in the back seat.

"Do you have a condom?" she asked.

"Do you have a condom?" he mimicked.

He turned her around, and she felt herself revolving awkwardly, like a rolled-up rug. She was facing the seat, and before she knew what to expect, it was already happening. Her tongue might pop out of her mouth, and her ribs would never unclench. She closed her eyes, and when she did that, she became, at the same time that she was Michelle, a pulseless object being stuffed and grabbed at. She squeezed her face up, so it felt as small and tight as a gum wrapper. She allowed it. He was Russell, and he wanted her. Russell made a choking sound, and then he lay on top of her, still inside of her, and she couldn't move. Then he pulled out.

"Slut," he said, pinching her nipple. Her throat flexed, but made no sound. "Good girl," he said, stroking her hair. She was thirsty from the Pepsi, from Russell, from everything she hadn't been able to say.

She sat up. The word slut repeated in her head like a car hitting a cement wall over and over again.

He seemed tired as he pulled his clothes on. The moon made everything visible, the traces of sweat on his shoulders, her white legs and hands, her hips. She tugged her underwear on, clipped her bra, and fixed her dress, then climbed over the front seat to the passenger's side. She slid her feet into her sandals.

Michelle flipped down the mirror and put on her Mysterious Red. Putting it on now had something to do with returning to who she was, locking herself up, but her face looked oddly tilted.

"You look garish with that on."

"Garish?"

"Freaky. It doesn't suit you."

The Golf heaved along the pot-holed dirt road.

She hoped that her mother would not be up, sitting stiffly upright at the end of the couch, the lamp shining on her short, curly light hair. Tonight, Michelle might cry, but she would not be able to say why. Her mother could stay awake as long as she wanted if it meant she could speak harshly to Michelle when she came in, trying to control her every move, her mind. When Michelle went out with Shannon and Tanya at night, tearing around the neighbourhood, going to parties—Michelle got all her As without trying—her mother would always be up and waiting, her gold watch still on her wrist. Michelle would go in to say goodnight, trying to stand straight, trying not to vomit, and her mother would ask in her foggy, late-night voice if she knew she was going to throw her life away, that she had better be using protection. Michelle told her she wasn't stupid, and that the last thing she wanted was a squawking baby. Her mother told her to never forget that every man Michelle met would try to take something away from her. She said men were lousy, hungry thieves, that's the way it was, and that's the way it would always be.

"What about love?" Michelle asked once. It was one of the songs she turned up full blast, so she could not hear her own voice singing.

"Garbage," her mother said, if she had had her full three glasses of French Cross. She once told her that men did not have souls, one arm flinging out into the air, like the arm of an actress in the middle of a stage.

The lights in her house were all out. Perhaps her mother had given up on Michelle. Her face scrunched up, and she bit hard on the inside of her cheek.

Michelle looked at Russell, waiting for him to say something, to apologize for doing what he did, whatever it was.

"Thanks," he said. "See you tomorrow. You have the key?"

She nodded. The conversation, which had never really started, was over.

He put the car in reverse, and she opened the door and got out. She knew how to get out of cars and not look back.

He drove away without waiting to see if she got inside. The summer cold bit and nipped at her arms. The dress was weak. The dress was nothing.

Inside, she slipped her feet out of the sandals. She put them neatly back in the closet, beside her mother's white pumps. The pumps matched the pink, papery dress her mother wore every morning to work. She locked the front door, turning the latch to the right. The house was quiet and dark, a tomb with pictures on the wall. Perhaps her mother had decided, finally, that she had said all that could be said, that Michelle was on her own.

Although she was thirsty, Michelle travelled like a ghost to her room. She looked in the closet mirror, the one she assessed herself in every morning, until her face looked perfect. But tonight she saw her slightly but fatally flawed face; her mouth looked like a sore, the red lipstick too striking for her normal features. Did she look like a bird? She didn't want to know, because she could only know so much before she didn't want to live. The dress hung loosely on her body. She went to her bedroom window and looked out at her backyard. She wanted to feel good again. Her eyes gradually adjusted to the darkness, and she could see the white lawn chairs—one designated hers and one designated her mother's. On rare occasions, they sat out on Saturday afternoons, very peacefully. It was when her mother seemed to allow herself to enjoy the world. She'd rest her arms on the chair and close her eyes, tilt her head up to the sun.

Early this summer, Michelle had said, "I think my life's going to get better and better."

Her mother giggled. She liked to think that because she suffered, because she'd let everything be stolen, that she was wise. But Michelle would never be wise, because she didn't want to be and didn't need to be. Everywhere she went, she thought, someone would want to have sex with her, someone would want to pry her open, see what was inside. She would be the one who decided if she wanted them back.

She listened, but her mother did not stir. He had dropped her off and driven away. He was on the 401, sucking Jujubes.

The night had grown truly cold. A cold night in the middle of summer, one that passed too soon, without the right things happening. Michelle rested her arms on the sill and watched as the goose bumps formed on her bare skin, seemingly all at once, at some inner, automatic command. She lifted her eyes. The geraniums her mother planted every spring slept in the garden. Although she could hardly see their red heads, she craned her neck, trying to smell their subtle sweetness.

Something Happy

CARMEN SNIPPED THROUGH THE cellophane that protected the orchid. Tonight, after grocery shopping, she had told Jason to park the Honda in front of the new flower shop that had opened up around a corner from their building. Inside, Jason had lingered by the jades, but Carmen had found the orchids, which stood all together on a table like regal, aristocratic women who had been cruelly frozen in the prime of their power, tags dangling. She brought an orchid to the counter, slapped down her debit card. She would put the orchid in the windowsill by the dining room table.

Carmen crumpled the cellophane and shoved it into the trash. As she filled a glass with water, she peered out the kitchen window. Jason and Carmen's eight-storey apartment building faced two beige office buildings owned by Imperial Oil, but behind them was the cemetery, a narrow tract of land, the gravestones slumped in snow. Last winter, Jason had skied along the paths, and Carmen had walked behind him.

She and Jason had just bought a house and would be leaving their apartment in the spring. She wondered if she would miss the apartment. Her mother and stepfather were on their way over from the west end of Toronto to have dinner to celebrate.

She dribbled water into the dry potting mix, then set the orchid on the windowsill. Jason, who had gone out to get butter for the squash he would bake, came in the door, his cheeks red. He tossed his keys on Carmen's desk, which was squeezed beside the kitchen and the vestibule, like something no one wanted but that couldn't be properly disposed of.

"Why are you putting it there?" he said, standing with his coat on, the block of butter in a bag.

"So it will get light."

"But there it will get too much light."

"What do you know about orchids?"

Without taking his coat or boots off, he marched across the parquet that Carmen had mopped the night before. He picked up the orchid and carried it like something breakable over to the coffee table, where an African Violet cramped its style.

"I had to go all the way to Loblaws," he said, and began to unbutton his coat.

"I have to clean the bathroom."

"You haven't started that yet?"

"No, I haven't."

Jason didn't say anything, just came close to her and rubbed both of her arms, as if to comfort her.

Carmen got down on her knees on the white tile floor where their short and long dark hairs snaked. She would wash the walls, too, because Jason insisted on thoroughness, and it wasn't that she was afraid to disappoint him, but that he was thorough with whatever he promised to do, and she didn't like being accused of not doing her share. None of the doctors had told her she couldn't clean. She just couldn't do yoga, swim, jog, do crunches, or drink coffee—Carmen was high-risk.

She didn't want to see her mother, who had become almost unrecognizable in the last year or so, since she retired. She had worked in a bank, selling mortgages and loans. Now she told Carmen she didn't walk outside because it was either too cold, too dark, or, in the summer, too oppressive. Carmen suggested she keep busy, rock babies at Sick Kids or speak English with immigrants. Over the phone, sitting in her quiet kitchen, her mother had said, "I'll think about it, Carmen." When Carmen was younger, her mother was a blur of hectic motion or she was flat on the couch, recovering.

Jason's family had donated the money for the down payment on the house. Both of his two older sisters already had houses and toddlers, though neither of them worked. Carmen and Jason both worked—Carmen was a graphic designer, Jason a history and economics teacher. The house they had finally bought sat in a field just outside of Guelph. The Victorian farmhouse was red brick with a green painted porch that listed to one side. A tree with sparse yellow leaves stood in the front yard. On their visit in the autumn, the real estate agent told Jason and Carmen that the owner, an elderly man, had died in the house. It didn't bother Carmen. Graduation and wedding photos of his son and daughter had lined the white plaster wall going up the narrow, creaking stairs to the top floor. Carmen studied the young, smiling faces until Jason put his knuckles gently in her back. Upstairs there were three small bedrooms. While Jason and the real estate agent discussed the drafty windows in the master bedroom, Carmen stood in the bedroom with pink walls, then wandered into the one with blue walls. They signed all the papers that the real estate agent, Lana, faxed to Carmen's office, and within a couple of weeks, the house was theirs to pay off for the rest of their lives.

"Carmen!"

She wrung the rag, then let it hang over the side of the tub. She got up carefully. In the medicine cabinet mirror, her face was already plump.

She stood and waited in the kitchen doorway. The small window was steamed up, and Jason was wearing the blue-and-white apron his mother had sent him in the mail for his birthday. Jason was leaning over a pan, stirring. The uncooked chicken thighs dressed in rosemary, thyme, and lemon basked crudely on the counter. Jason turned, cupping his palm beneath a spoonful of liquid.

"Taste this," he said, and the up-close sage smell made Carmen gag, but she opened her lips for the spoon.

She sipped it. "Too strong," she said.

"That's what I thought."

She turned to go back to the bathroom.

"Carmen."

"Yes?"

"We'll have a good time tonight."

"Yeah."

"You really want the orchid in the front?"

"It looks better there."

He moved past her without hostility, picked the orchid up, and carried it over to the windowsill where the petals would probably burn in the February sunlight.

By the time Carmen was back in the bathroom, the sage smell was no longer upsetting her stomach. Carmen rinsed the rag with too-hot water and wrung it out. She could hear Jason whistling. The two of them had gone years before they met each other's families. They had lived in the dark, slanting rain on the West Coast, and all of their time was their own. Weekends and evenings, they burrowed deeply in their apartment, under the duvet, watching rented films all day, and rising only to eat and go to the bathroom, or they went for soggy, sloshy drives in Carmen's '87 Toyota, the engine set to rev high so that it wouldn't stall at red lights. But could they always live like that? There were steps, weren't there? Then she and Jason had married a year after returning to Ontario. They had planned to elope, but Jason's mother begged him to have a wedding. Jason's eldest sister arranged Carmen's shower, which she held at her house in Aurora, in a room dotted with yellow chrysanthemums. On the day of their wedding, neither Carmen nor Jason could get out of bed—they lay quietly, not asleep, not awake. Then Jason turned over, rested his hand across Carmen's stomach, and said, "It's just one day out of our lives." He told her they would get through it, and everything would go back to normal. People would no longer gather around them with gifts and encouragement and questions.

Jason was singing now as he banged a spoon against a pot. This meant he was in a good mood, and Carmen was relieved. He wouldn't be so picky about the bathroom, and lecture her about standards. Instead, he was gleefully making a meal that would impress Carmen's family, making them look at Carmen like she really had gotten lucky.

Carmen's mother was wearing the red scarf Carmen had knitted her the year before. Her mother always wrapped it around her neck despite the fact that Carmen had dropped a stitch and didn't know how to fix it, so she left the hole. As her mother handed her her coat, Carmen smelled Very Irrésistible, the perfume her mother always wore, and she grew nauseous. Now there was nowhere safe from the innocent smells of the world, smells she used to like. Harold, her stepfather, handed Carmen the black coat he had worn since she was a teenager. He could have bought a new one—he had been an air traffic controller—but he thought that if something was perfectly okay, only a little misshapen, there was no need to replace it. He patted her shoulder. Harold and Carmen liked each other, but they never hugged. Carmen hung up their coats in the small front closet where Jason's back-country skis leaned. Jason scolded her the first time her mother and Harold visited the apartment when Carmen had laid their coats on an empty chair.

Carmen's mother and Harold both sat on the couch facing the fireplace. The apartment building was one of the first Art Deco buildings in Toronto. The fireplace mantel was white, and the inside was empty and black. When Carmen and Jason moved in, a mirror was leaned up against the back wall of the fireplace, and they decided to leave it there to make the room look even larger.

Carmen sat on the chair facing the couch, the position that offered a view of the kitchen and her desk tucked into a corner. It suddenly occurred to her that she was overdue for a visit with her father. It was like a whack to the head, remembering. She talked to her father four times a year—much more than some of her friends spoke to their fathers. Neither her mother nor her father knew Carmen's news.

"I always have trouble with orchids," her mother said. She had turned her entire body to see the orchid better.

"Do you read the instructions?" Carmen asked, and Jason turned from the stove and frowned at her. She was always left to entertain while he cooked.

"I give them full sun, and they die anyway."

Carmen's mother squinted out the window at the city, all the buildings unevenly lit up.

"So when's the big move?"

"April first," Carmen said.

"And hopefully you won't live to regret it," Harold said. All the while they were house-hunting, he told them not to buy, to enjoy apartment living. He told them he'd never won on real estate.

"Too bad you couldn't just buy this place," her mother said. On the day she moved into this apartment, Carmen had told her that she wanted to live there—with its view of the city, the high ceilings, the beautiful fireplace—for the rest of her life. Sometimes she confided these lush secrets to her mother, then wished she hadn't. Her mother often held them against her, unwilling to imagine that Carmen could change her mind.

Outside, a streetcar was rattling by. In their new house, there would be the silence of fields and layers of dark and cold.

Everyone was quiet for a moment, likely, Carmen thought, because the most logical thing to talk about next was the money, but Jason had warned her not to bring up the topic. It made him feel pathetic that his family had to help them, that they would be apartment dwellers forever if it weren't for his family. Carmen's mother and Harold kept money separate.

"How's Arnie?" Carmen said.

"Well, now she wants to move to Erin. Take the kids for the summer."

"He should say no," Carmen said.

"I told him."

Arnold was Carmen's brother. Last year, his wife left him and her two children, and she was now seven months pregnant with a salesman's child. Carmen thought it was all so seedy, but was a neatly bordered life so much better? Her brother ran through all the steps half-blind, yet he was surviving.

"I could have told you on the wedding day what that marriage would amount to," Harold said, and nobody said anything. He always had to know everything.

"He's a good father," Carmen's mother said. "And a catch."

"How are the girls?"

"Justine might not get her year. That's what Arn said."

"What about Mandy?"

"Fine."

"How on earth could she be fine?"

"Arnold's a good father."

Jason popped his head out from the kitchen. "Anyone want wine?"

Harold said, "Yes, sir," which meant Carmen's mother would be driving home, even though she hated navigating the city even in daylight. Harold couldn't resist wine.

"And how are your parents?" Carmen's mother asked.

Jason came out with a bottle of wine and a glass, his apron still on. "They're in Ireland," he said.

"Hopefully they come back in one piece," Harold said.

"That's all over, Harold," Carmen's mother said. "Don't be so embarrassing."

"I haven't heard from them," Jason said, smiling as if he hadn't heard what her mother said. "So I guess that's a good sign." He filled Harold's glass, took the bottle back to the kitchen.

"So when are you going to start packing?" Carmen's mother said, perking up, as if she were remembering something exciting. Her mother's hairdresser had dyed her eyebrows a golden brown to match her hair. Her mother peered out from underneath them.

From the kitchen, Jason looked at Carmen, who said, "Don't look at me."

And then no one spoke, and Carmen could guess what her mother was thinking—that Carmen was just as snappish with Jason as she always had been with her. Before they got married, Carmen's mother told Jason that Carmen disagreed for the sake of disagreeing. "So she was warning you?" Carmen said, and she tossed her head back and didn't exactly laugh. "She's kind of right," Jason had said. And Carmen threw her book down, beginning a whole afternoon of defensive manoeuvring and useless explaining. Carmen disagreed to survive. What hyperbole, Jason had said.

"It'll be nice for you two," her mother said. "A new start."

"It'll be nice to have space," Jason said, removing the squash from the oven.

"I've never had much use for space," Harold said. "It's overrated."

Harold always had to know everything, and he always had to contradict. Carmen's mother rolled her eyes at him. She'd only started doing that since she retired.

"You'll have to find a new doctor. New hairdresser," her mother said, looking out at the view again.

"I'm going to keep the ones I have," Carmen said.

Jason hung his apron on a hook by the doorway. "That's a bit silly," he said, and he did his nervous cough-laugh.

"The two most important people in a woman's life. Her doctor and her hairdresser," Carmen's mother said.

Harold reached over and tousled her mother's hair, but when he removed his hand, her hair looked the same.

Jason served the meal—roasted butternut squash with sage butter, the dressed-up chicken thighs, a salad with blue cheese and pears. Everyone ate with their napkins in their laps, something Carmen's family had done only in restaurants or at Thanksgiving, Christmas, or Easter dinner when they sat at the dining room table with the good silverware. The red wine was in the middle of the table, but only Jason and Harold drank. If anyone asked why Carmen wasn't drinking, the answer was that she was taking antibiotics for an ear infection. Carmen's mother and Harold murmured amazement at the delicious food. There were the usual jokes about how Carmen could not cook, how her mother tried to teach her, but Carmen refused to even peel a potato. "Women's lib, mom," her mother mimicked.

Carmen was in charge of dessert. She took the store-bought cherry cheesecake—Jason's favourite, which he had not eaten before meeting Carmen—out of the fridge. Jason had taught her to slice it evenly, and how to transfer the cake from the cardboard platter to the plate without demolishing it. The first time they had his parents over, months and months ago, he had taught her not to cut the pieces too big. "We're not barbarians," he had said.

Everyone dug into the cake, but Carmen just looked at hers. She couldn't eat it, the red and white mush; it was suddenly vile, disgusting. She held the fork in her hand and looked out the window. When she turned to her mother, her mother smiled at her, but Carmen did not smile back.

Carmen and Jason made coffee together, but Carmen didn't get down a cup for herself. She would use the same excuse for coffee that she used for wine. They took the carafe from the cupboard, the cream and sugar dishes Jason had bought, and served it. Cups with saucers—Jason's training. Carmen's mother had two cups. She sipped, set her cup down, sipped, set her cup down.

"Who wants to go for a walk?" Harold asked, clapping his hands together.

Another tradition in Carmen's family was to walk after dinner—Harold knew because he'd been in the family since Carmen was eight. The family didn't walk after regular weeknight suppers, but after celebratory, holiday dinners. They would walk no matter what the weather was like. If they were at Carmen's grandparents' house, Carmen's grandmother would go downstairs to her cold basement where no one ever spent time (unlike in the houses where Carmen grew up, where basements were for ping-pong, board hockey, jamming, movies in the VCR, and birthday parties with pizza, spin-the-bottle, and chocolate cake). Her grandmother would bring up one of her grandfather's heavy wool coats, and Carmen would wear it over her own, plus one of her grandmother's knitted hats. Once her grandmother made her wear her grandfather's grey work socks over her city mittens. The family would weave together along empty roads like a pack of gentle animals, and the icy snow would burn Carmen's cheeks.

Jason handed everyone their coats, hats, gloves, and scarves. Carmen's mother took her purse with her.

In the elevator, Carmen's mother stood in the corner, looking down. The fluorescent lights made the small blue mole in the upper corner of her mother's forehead clearer and more malignant-looking. The mole had been there for years, never growing. Jason put his arm around Carmen, so they were the only ones touching. Carmen had never seen Harold casually put his arm around her mother. When Carmen was a child, he was more likely to grab her mother from behind and wrestle her to the ground, leading Carmen to stop whatever she was doing and stiffly leave the room.

The mild winter air was disappointing. The chill of Carmen's childhood winters had made her feet and hands and mouth ache with cold, but then there was the return to warmth, the thawing, the cuddling with her grandfather in his easy chair. Carmen plucked off her hat and stuffed it in her pocket. A mild winter night with a wind from the south. If the wind kept coming, holes would form in the snow, which would become long, dirty puddles.

"Hey," Jason said. "Let's walk through the cemetery."

Outside, Carmen's mother looked smaller, and Carmen couldn't help but think of her mother's death. At her grandmother's funeral, after the burial, on the way back to the car, Carmen's mother had dropped to her knees in the grass.

"Oh, I love cemeteries," her mother said.

"You've always been a spooky one," Harold said. Every once in a while, her mother had a dream that came true. When Carmen lost a watch her father had given to her, her mother said she dreamt it was underneath a blanket, and then Carmen found it under her blankets down near the foot of the bed. She slept with it on.

Harold took her mother's hand. Maybe they walked like that all the time; how would Carmen know now?

The cemetery was an old one from the 1800s, no longer in use. It lay behind the Imperial Oil buildings. When Jason started back-country skiing last year, he'd warmed up his body and his equipment by skiing in the cemetery after dinner. Carmen had walked behind him because she didn't want to be in the apartment alone while he skied in the cemetery. Carmen smiled—they were only trying then.

Because the gates were always locked at night, they had to cross at the lights and then cut across the Imperial Oil building's parking lot. They had to climb over a metal fence, then hop down about two feet. Jason helped Carmen's mother. Carmen watched Harold carefully to make sure he did not put out his back. When Carmen was eleven, he'd put his back out in the bathtub, and her mother had had to call an ambulance. Carmen hid in her room, but she peeked out when the paramedics carried him out on a stretcher. He looked like a deer that had been shot but was not bleeding.

Then the four of them walked on the snow, soft and creaking, in and among the gravestones. Carmen found the moon through the leafless trees: a mirror looking into its own shining mirror face. At first, the four of them walked in a line, and then Jason and Harold drifted ahead—they really were like father and son, but without any expectations of each other or disappointments to mourn. Harold's son hadn't lived with him since he was eight, and now he lived in Japan with his wife and baby son. Jason's father still didn't understand why Jason dropped out of law school and applied to teacher's college.

Her mother stopped, slouched as she dug into her purse. Then she slid out her package of Vantage Lights, popped out the tray, and pulled out a cigarette. She flicked the lighter and lit it on the first try. The flame was an inch high.

Her mother inhaled deeply. She'd had to wait all through dinner because Carmen hadn't offered to open a window, as she did in the summer, and Jason must have forgotten to offer.

Her mother started walking again, and Carmen followed. Their walk through the snow was more of a meander.

"Whenever I'm in a graveyard," her mother said, "I think of how silly it all is."

"What?"

"All the fanfare. Just bury me."

"Don't say that."

Her mother laughed her low laugh, as she did when Carmen turned away from anything sexual she might have said. When Carmen was a girl, her mother never neglected to say, "My period's heavy this month."

"As natural as birth, just the opposite direction."

"I don't want to think about it."

"No? I guess I didn't much either when I was your age."

They walked for a while not saying anything, and Carmen deeply wanted to tell her mother the news, but the words stayed inside.

"How's work?" her mother asked. "That lady still giving you a hard time?"

Carmen nodded.

"She'll get her day," her mother said, but Carmen wasn't sure.

"I always thought you'd be an actress. I could see you winning an Academy Award."

Carmen had taken an improv class the summer she was sixteen, and her mother never dropped the idea of Carmen becoming an actress.

"But don't all mothers think that about their daughters?"

Carmen looked at her mother. The wind had not changed the shape of her hair but had puffed it up, like a hen's feathers. The moonlight showed the smoker's wrinkles branching around her eyes and mouth, which Carmen hadn't noticed in the apartment's dim light. What did her mother see when she looked at Carmen? Carmen was thirty-six, on the other side of youth, and could only hope for so much now.

"You were always different," her mother said, her voice thinly bright.

Yes, her mother always said that Carmen was special, somehow destined, but something had gone wrong. She could have been many things—an actress, a lawyer, an artist—but the only thing Carmen wanted badly was her own safe future.

They walked, and her mother puffed away on her cigarette. Jason and Harold were up ahead, two black coats, two men, one just barely stooping, the one who had once renovated her mother's basement without any help. The sound of the saw and hammer had forced Carmen into her room, away from the television and back to her pencil designs and her thoughts.

"I hope Arnie finds someone," Carmen said.

"Me, too," her mother said.

"But at least he's learning how to cook."

"I just hope the person he finds next is more understanding."

"Understanding of what?"

"Who he is," her mother said sternly, as if the new woman were standing right there.

"But Arnie needs to learn how to understand people, too," Carmen said. "It's a two-way street."

"He tried with that woman," her mother said. "She acted like a bloody teenager about everything." Her mother stopped, took a puff of her cigarette, then dropped it in the snow, pressed the tip of her boot on it. After Carmen's parents divorced, her father used to piggy-back Carmen to the mall and talk about her mother. As Carmen held tightly onto his neck, he told her that her mother spoiled Arnold, wouldn't scold him or spank him when he stuck his tongue out at a cashier or peed in the sink. "Wouldn't treat him like a normal kid," he said. When Carmen's dad bought a motorcycle, her mother wouldn't let Arnold ride on the back, but she would let Carmen. Carmen's mother was always afraid Arnold would suddenly die. He didn't get his driver's licence until he moved out, and although he did get into an accident, he only banged his head on the steering wheel and didn't die. One of Carmen's brothers did die a week after he was born, before Arnold and Carmen were ever thought of or needed. He was buried in a cemetery in Scarborough—no one ever visited—and his name was Donald Junior. Her mother told her the story once, when Carmen was twelve. They were driving home from Carmen's grandparents' house, just the two of them, she couldn't remember why. Her mother shared the grim story, her voice hoarse, but never told it again. Every once in a while, Carmen remembered her infant brother's brief existence.

Carmen was getting cold; maybe the air wasn't as mild as she thought. And she was suddenly very tired, tired and strangely tearful.

Sometimes there was tipsy excitement, and sometimes there was its exact opposite—exhaustion, the need to sleep, sadness heavy as earth. She tried to think of something happy—the house, the new Volvo Jason talked about leasing, the playpen folded under the bed (which Jason said they had bought too soon but which Carmen had made him pay for—he made more money than her).

Jason and Harold had reached the front gate and were circling back around. When Carmen had walked behind Jason when he skied, she never let him out of her sight, get around a corner without her. She wouldn't have gotten lost, she knew that. The fear was irrational, but Carmen had listened to it.

"Oh look, another Emily." Then her mother said, "That one's really made a comeback."

Carmen nodded.

"I have your grandmother's china for you," her mother said. "She took good care of it."

"I don't really have room for it," Carmen said. She suddenly saw her grandmother's hands—solid and covered in age spots.

"But you will," her mother said. Carmen heard a strain in her mother's voice, but when Carmen looked, her mother was not exactly smiling, but looking up and off at something pleasant only she could see.

By the time they reached the metal fence, Carmen was happy to see Jason, how young and strong he was; they still had so much before them, she was sure. There was so much to hope for and nothing would go wrong. Jason helped Harold and then Carmen's mother up onto the low, concrete wall, then up and over the fence.

They crossed the street, not bothering to walk over to the lights. The neighbourhood emptied at night; all the office workers went home and all the old, rich people went to sleep.

There was no reason for them to go back inside. There was nothing to say or do after the walk, the last stage of the ritual. Harold and her mother stopped outside the car. Her mother was shivering, something Carmen hadn't noticed during the walk. The scarf Carmen had knit was hanging down.

"Let's get home," Harold said. "Take care." He lifted his hand in a wave. Then he got in the driver's side and Carmen didn't remind him about the three glasses of wine he had drunk. Her mother hugged Jason, then Carmen, whispering, "I love you." She only ever whispered those words.

Carmen and Jason waved as the car rolled away. Maybe her mother hadn't wanted to know.

They went back inside their building and stood outside the elevator. The door opened, and Jason let Carmen step inside first. The elevator walls were a dull, not unpleasing, yellow. She leaned against Jason. Her breasts were sore, but Jason smelled good to her, warm, faintly sweet. She wished everything was over.

The lights were still on the in the apartment, so the mess left on the dining room table glared, offended. They took off their boots and coats. Carmen didn't want to wake up to a mess. She never felt well in the mornings, but she didn't really feel well now either. Her doctor, who spooned yogurt into her mouth as she scanned Carmen's file, had told her nausea was a good sign, that hormone levels were in order. She tried to imagine the embryo—she refused to call it anything else— but what came into her mind when she closed her eyes was a young girl, one Carmen had never seen, tobogganing. The child thriving and living was too much to hope for, but Carmen couldn't help it. The room was waiting, the house was waiting, the childhood that Carmen would oversee and guide was waiting.

Carmen scraped plates into the garbage. She should call Arnold to see if he was still surviving. Even if she called him to make him feel better, he would always say, "Everything's going to be okay, Carmen. Don't worry so much." The words worked for everything—breakups, failures, flat discouragement.

Jason came up behind her and put his arms around her. This was the new thing he was doing. Carmen didn't know what to make of it or even if she liked it. She wriggled, and he let go. "Fine," he said.

The nausea began ballooning inside her. The scraps of squash skin and chicken bones and crumbs of cake…she closed the lid of the garbage bin and closed her eyes to the mess on the counter. She rested her hand on her belly. Nothing could be seen yet, but her belly had a new firmness.

Then, thinking it might help, she crossed the threshold of the kitchen into the living room. An old friend had told her that if you crossed a threshold into another room, you forgot what you were thinking about in the previous room. Maybe Carmen could leave the nausea in the kitchen.

Jason was sitting at the dining room table and looking out at the Imperial Oil buildings across the street. A giant oak tree used to soften the hardness of the buildings, but the city had cut the tree down to a stump. Carmen sat down beside Jason, in the chair her mother had occupied. No one had noticed or talked about the orchid during dinner, the way Carmen had intended. She didn't know what she wanted anyone to say. She only wanted it to be the centre of something, to hold something together that she herself couldn't hold together. A distraction, maybe. But now the orchid looked hunched, not like a regal aristocrat at all. It looked like something much too delicate, almost abnormal and alien, the petals too pink, as if it were gasping for air.

Acknowledgments

I would like to thank the Canada Council for the Arts and the Toronto Arts Council for financial support. I am also grateful to Belinda Fernandes, BSW, Anne Sheehan, MSW, RSW, and Vera Pellet, RN, for pertinent information and insight.

I would like to express my profound thanks to everyone at Arsenal Pulp Press, including Brian Lam, Susan Safyan, and Gerilee McBride for their incredible energy and optimism and their editorial care with these stories. The fiercely determined and indefatigable Carolyn Swayze also deserves my gratitude. I am indebted to Catherine Graham; many of these stories benefited from her extraordinary skills and talents. Sandra Campbell also provided razor-sharp advice and, along with Catherine Graham, played a crucial role in helping this collection make its way uphill. Tim Mitchell also lent me his keen eye and instinct for story. Thank you to Amber Lin for the haven of the writing hours.

I would like to thank my family, in particular my sister, Sander Deeth, for her bright and constant faith in me and my writing. Last and most of all, I would like to thank Liam Baldwin for accompanying me, with his resolute confidence and wisdom, across all terrain and through all weather.

Kelli Deeth's first book, *The Girl Without Anyone*, was chosen as one of *The Globe and Mail*'s Best Books of 2001. Her stories have been published in various journals and anthologies including *Write Turns, Event, The Dalhousie Review, The Puritan*, and *Joyland*. She holds an MFA in creative writing from the University of British Columbia and currently lives in Toronto, where she teaches creative writing at the University of Toronto. *kellideeth.net*